hink maybe you're thinking…
issing me."

"You do, huh?"

"Well. Are you?"

He crinkled his brow, as if deep in thought.

"Are you?" she demanded.

He smiled at her. Slowly. "As a matter of fact, I am."

He touched her chin. He traced the back of a finger down the side of her neck, just beneath the soft fall of her hair.

"I…um…" Tessa's breathing was agitated. "You shouldn't. Really."

"Yeah. I should."

He took her mouth. Because he *had* to kiss her. And also to make her stop telling him not to.

Available in March 2010
from Mills & Boon®
Special Moments™

THE STRANGER
AND TESSA JONES

BY
CHRISTINE RIMMER

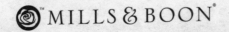

First published in Great Britain 2010
Harlequin Mills & Boon Limited,
Eton House, 18-24 Paradise Road, Richmond, Surrey TW9 1SR

© Christine Rimmer 2009

ISBN: 978 0 263 87955 1

23-0310

Harlequin Mills & Boon policy is to use papers that are natural, renewable
and recyclable products and made from wood grown in sustainable forests.
The logging and manufacturing processes conform to the legal environmental
regulations of the country of origin.

Printed and bound in Spain
by Litografia Rosés S.A., Barcelona

Christine Rimmer came to her profession the long way around. Before settling down to write about the magic of romance, she'd been everything from an actress to a salesclerk to a waitress. Now that she's finally found work that suits her perfectly, she insists she never had a problem keeping a job – she was merely gaining "life experience" for her future as a novelist. Christine is grateful not only for the joy she finds in writing, but for what waits when the day's work is through: a man she loves, who loves her right back, and the privilege of watching their children grow and change day to day.

She lives with her family in Oklahoma. Visit Christine at www.christinerimmer.com.

For Gail Chasan, my fabulous editor.
You are the best!

Chapter One

"More snow on the way." The truck driver, a fifty-something guy in insulated pants and a plaid flannel shirt, fiddled with the radio dial.

The man in the passenger seat made a low sound in his throat, a sound of agreement that discouraged further conversation. He had a killer headache. Talking only made it ache all the harder. And he kept smelling alcohol.

He sniffed the sleeve of his jacket. Definitely. Booze. Was he drunk? He didn't feel drunk, exactly. He just felt bad. Bad all over.

The two-lane road, dangerously slick in spots, treated with road salt and dotted with slushy ridges of brown snow, twisted and turned down the mountain. Piled snow, hard-packed and dirty, rose in twin walls to either side, so the big rig seemed to roll through a dingy white tunnel, a tunnel rimmed above with evergreens and roofed higher still by a steel-colored sky.

The passenger shut his eyes, tuned out the drone of the radio and leaned his pounding head against the seatback. For a while, he dozed. When he opened his eyes again, the walls of snow on either side had diminished. He spotted a sign that said this road was Scenic Highway 49.

With a hydraulic moan and hiss, the trucker slowed the rig as they came to a sharp turn. Another turn after that and they were slowing even more.

They passed an intersection, a road winding off into the tall trees, and then another. The passenger read the street sign at that second road: Rambling Lane. And Main Street. They were on Main Street. The two-lane highway had now become the central street of some hole-in-the-wall town.

Another turn in the road and they were rolling past a town hall and a one-room post office on the right. On the left, a café and a mountain bike shop and a store called Fletcher Gold Sales, followed by a couple of tourist-trap gift shops. The place was like something out of an old western movie—or maybe, thought the passenger, like a small town in Texas, except with everything crowded together and tall mountains all around.

Texas. The passenger frowned. *Am I from Texas?* No answer came to him. His head pounded harder.

"Welcome to North Magdalene, California, population two-thirty on a very busy day," said the driver, as he pulled the rig into a parking lot across from a restaurant called The Mercantile Grill, which was next-door to a bar fittingly named The Hole in the Wall. The hydraulic brakes sighed as they rolled to a stop in a long space surrounded by piles of gray snow. The driver flipped levers and worked the big gearshift. Finally, the huge truck was silent. "It's lunchtime and I skipped breakfast." The trucker scratched his chin. "I'm heading up the street to the café, get a quick burger to go, fill my thermos. Then I'm on to Grass Valley. I figure, just a little bit of luck and I'll make it before the road shuts down."

The passenger frowned. "Shuts down?"

The driver reminded him, "More snow comin', remember? Weatherman said the storm on the way's gonna be a doozy. Hungry?"

The passenger winced and touched the wound on his forehead. "Uh. Thanks. No."

The trucker shook his head. "Listen. I never like to mess in a man's business, but you don't look so good. There's a clinic a few miles from here. Come on with me to the café, I'll find someone to run you on over there and—"

"No." The passenger put up a hand, not sure why he didn't want to see a doctor—not sure of anything, really. Except that he wished his head would stop pounding and he really hoped he didn't throw up. "Thanks. I'll get off here." He leaned on the door and it opened. Icy air flowed in around him. He swung his legs over and jumped to the frozen blacktop, slipping in his smooth-soled boots—but catching himself in time to stay upright.

The trucker tried again to offer aid. "I got an extra coat in the back." He was leaning across the seat. "Let me get it for—"

"I'm fine. Thanks." The man shut the door on the driver and turned toward the sidewalk, not caring that he was headed back the way he'd come. It seemed as good a direction as any right then. Behind him, he heard the driver's door open and slam shut, but the trucker didn't call to him.

Good. The man flipped up the collar of his lightweight jacket, hunched down into it for what warmth it could provide, stuck his hands in his pockets and concentrated on crossing the ice-slick parking lot without landing on his ass.

He made it. The sidewalk, beneath the old-timey wooden cover, was dry. He walked faster, keeping his eyes focused downward, careful not to make eye contact with the few bundled-up people he passed. His headache beat a jarring accompaniment to each step he took and his stomach roiled.

Too soon, he was leaving the gift shops and the bike store behind, emerging from under the sidewalk cover and into the open. Now he was unprotected from the punishing wind that blew against his face like frozen needles and quickly penetrated the thin fabric of his jacket and his slacks. He had to watch every step. The boots he looked down on were expensive. But they weren't made for trekking along the side of an icy road. His feet were cold and getting wet, his toes like lumps of ice. His body ached, in a whole bunch of different places. Like he'd taken a serious beating. His tan slacks were torn at the knees, the fabric bloody from cuts beneath. And his jacket not only stank of booze, it was streaked with black marks that might have been grease or oil or maybe plain dirt. It had a rip down one side.

Whatever the hell had happened to him, it must have been bad.

The occasional pickup or SUV went past. Sometimes the drivers honked. The man had a feeling if he'd signaled one of them, they would have stopped.

But then there would be talking. And questions. The man didn't want any questions. After all, he had no answers. Questions made his head hurt worse. They were black holes he might fall into and never get out.

He forged on, passing Rambling Lane again. When he reached that other tree-shaded road farther up, he stood for a moment staring blankly at the street sign: Locust Street. With a shrug he started down it, thinking that it might be warmer within the relative protection of the evergreens.

It wasn't. The trees cut the wind, yes, but the shadowed spaces beneath the spreading branches seemed colder, somehow, than the open road. A cold that seeped into his bones.

What the hell was he doing? How had he gotten here?

He no sooner thought the questions than the pain in his head bloomed into agony. His breath hissed in and out through his clenched teeth. "No questions," he chanted in a whisper. "No answers. Don't ask…"

Wallet.

The word came into his mind and he paused on the shadowed, snow-drifted road. Of course. If he had a wallet, he might learn his name, at least. And where he lived….

Hope rising, he felt in his pockets with numb fingers. First in the jacket, then in the back pockets of his pants….

Nothing.

He even unzipped the jacket to look for a hidden pocket. There was one. Too bad it was as empty as the others. He saw the soft sweater he wore. It was streaked with grime like the jacket. Blue. The right word for what the sweater was made of came to him: cashmere.

Expensive, he thought, zipping back up again. He had that gash on his forehead and various other bruises and scrapes. And no wallet. No watch or rings, either. No jewelry of any kind. His clothes were the best quality, but all wrong for a frozen winter day high in the mountains.

California, the truck driver had said. He was in California. In the mountains.

The Sierras, he thought, and almost smiled. Even though the pain in his head continued, it didn't instantly jump to a screaming throb. *I'm in the Sierra Mountains of California, in or near a town called North Magdalene.*

"Could be worse," he mumbled. "I could be dead...." That struck him as funny, for some unknown reason. He started to laugh.

But then the ice-pick jabs of pain attacked his head again. His stomach lurched and rolled. He bent at the knees, braced his hands on his thighs and sucked in air, blowing it out hard, in steaming puffs, willing the agony in his head to fade to an aching throb and his stomach to stop churning.

A sudden image filled his mind: Early morning. Cold. Astride a horse that chuffed and shook a dark mane. High desert prairie stretched out around him, shadowed but for the slender ribbon of orange sun at the horizon. Someone beside him, also on horseback. He turned to look and see who it was...

The image vanished.

He closed his eyes and let out a low moan as he forced himself to rise from his crouch. The pain, which came in waves that swelled and diminished, was backing off again and his stomach had settled down. He lifted his face to the dark trees overhead.

Snow. As the truck driver had predicted. On his cheeks. His brows. His eyelids. He opened his eyes. Yes. Snowing. Hard enough now that it even found its way through the dense canopy of evergreen above his head.

And the wind was picking up, rustling the branches of the trees, making high-pitched moaning sounds. He started walking again, putting his head down, doggedly, into the wind, staggering a little in the deepening drifts, pondering the idea that he was probably going to die and just cold and miserable and hurting enough that death was starting to seem like a welcome relief.

But then, out of nowhere, he heard the strangest sound. He paused in mid-stride and cocked his head, listening, not sure if the sound was inside his head.

But no. There it came again—something shattering. Pottery or glass or…dishes.

Someone was breaking dishes? Deep in the Sierras in the middle of a snowstorm?

The white flakes whirled around him. And then he heard a voice.

"Bill. How could you?" A woman's voice. Another dish exploded. And another after that. "I hate you, Bill. You lied to me." More dinnerware crashed against what was probably the trunk of a tree.

Forgetting for the moment about encroaching death, almost certain he must be losing what remained of his mind, he left the road to forge into the trees and get closer to the bizarre sounds. It seemed crucial, for some reason, to see for himself if there was really a woman out here in the middle of nowhere, a woman throwing dishes and ranting at some guy named Bill.

Not far into the trees, he stopped. Maybe thirty yards from where he stood, the trees ended in a clearing. At the far edge of the clear space, he saw a small, wood-sided house with a steep, red tin roof, smoke spiraling skyward from a gray metal chimney pipe. He sniffed. The smell of woodsmoke came to him sharply. He should have noticed it before.

And there really was a woman. She was alone, as far as he could tell, and standing at a point about midway between the edge of the trees and the house. No sign of the guy she was yelling at. Just her and a big box of dishes near her snow-booted feet, and her target: a broad-trunked cedar tree.

Littering the fallen snow at the base of the tree were a thousand shards of broken pottery in a variety of bright colors, all swiftly being buried by the increasingly heavy fall of new snow.

Sudden dizziness assailed the man, accompanied by another bout of powerful nausea. He braced himself against the nearest tree. Blinking to clear his head, gulping to keep from hurling whatever he had in his stomach onto the pure, white snow, he focused on the woman.

She was tall. A big woman, not fat, but…sturdy. Probably in her twenties. She wore a purple quilted jacket and a striped knit hat with a pom-pom on top. Tendrils of blond hair escaped from under the hat, clinging to her red cheeks and bunching at her collar. Beside her, the cardboard box held plenty more dishes where the ones she'd thrown had come from. They were all different colors, those dishes. A rainbow of dinnerware waiting at her feet.

As he gulped down his nausea and blinked to try and clear the dizziness, she bent and grabbed up a plate the color of a sunflower. "You jerk!" She growled the words low in her throat. For a moment, he was sure she must be talking to him. But no. She stared into the middle distance, totally unaware of him. *Crash.* He winced as the plate hit the target and yellow shards went flying. She bent for another. "You promised. *Promised.*" She tossed a purple soup bowl. It found its mark and exploded. She grabbed two plates—turquoise and light green—one in each hand. "You said you'd be here for the wedding, Bill. I told everyone—*everyone*—that you were coming."

She fired one plate and then the other, so fast that the second hit the first. Bits of pottery flew in all directions.

"But no," she growled. "Oh, no. You couldn't just come to North Magdalene the way you always promised you would. Uh-uh. Instead, you took a little trip to Vegas to try your luck. Vegas…" A dark blue cup and a shamrock-green saucer met their end. "You fell in love with a showgirl. And she fell in love with you. A showgirl? You?" Another plate flew and shattered.

The man in the trees knew he shouldn't be hearing all this. He should show himself or go. But he did neither. He held on to a tree trunk to keep from passing out, as the big blonde in the clearing continued to rail at a guy who wasn't there.

"Tell me, Bill. How does a skinny tour bus driver with a space between his teeth, a guy too shy to string more than two sentences together in the presence of a woman, end up married to a showgirl? You tell me, Bill Toomey. How does that happen?" She fired three bread plates— white, black and orange—in swift succession.

As soon as the last one hit, she went on, "Especially when last September you swore, Bill, you *swore* with all your heart that you loved me." She threw a pink serving bowl. "*Me,* Bill." The snow swirled around her and the pom-pom on her hat bounced in sympathetic fury. The hair that curled along her cheeks blew across her eyes. She swiped it away and bent to grab more ammunition. "You swore you loved me and wanted to spend your life only at my side…" A cardinal-red dish met a crashing fate.

The man in the trees was frowning. He muttered, "Another damn drama queen," and wondered a second later why he'd said that.

And then he stepped forward, although some remnant of a survival instinct within him cautioned that it was unwise to approach a furious woman with a box full of dinnerware and an excellent throwing arm. She might choose *him* as her next target.

He walked toward her anyway, slowly at first and then faster, as the snow came down harder and the wind whistled in the branches of the tall, green trees. In seconds, as dishes continued to shatter and the big blonde with the bobbing pom-pom went on telling off some guy named Bill, he emerged from the shelter of the pines.

She'd just tossed a serving platter when she spotted him. A yelp of surprise escaped her. "What the…?" She reached into the box and came out with a second big platter. She waved it, a threat. "Stop. Don't come one step closer."

He kept coming. The platter was big and heavy-looking. If she hit him with it, it would probably make his headache a whole lot worse. But somehow, he couldn't stop moving toward her. "I need…I…Please…"

She raised the platter higher. "Final warning. Stop right there."

He croaked, "Don't…" as in his head a thousand bells began to ring. "Don't…" He put his hands over his ears, a move he knew to be pointless. There was no protecting his ears from the ringing. It was coming from inside his head. And the ice pick was stabbing in there again. He groaned as he felt himself slowly dropping to the ground.

It took forever to get there. It seemed to him that as the ice pick stabbed and stabbed again and the thousand bells kept pealing, he drifted downward—floating, like a leaf or maybe a feather.

Then, after forever, he found himself on his back in a thick drift of snow. He stared up at the gray sky, or tried to. But the snow was falling so hard by then, it was difficult to see more than a few feet above his face. The cold white flakes caught on his eyelashes. He blinked them away. The bells had gone silent. The ice pick had stopped its stabbing. A sigh of sweet relief escaped him.

Someone was beside him in the snow. The blonde. She was on her knees, looking down at him, bending closer. Her nose was as red as her cheeks with the cold. She smelled good. Fresh. Clean. Her breath, across his face, was warm and sweet.

As if it had happened long ago, he recalled her fury and the shattering dishes, the way she'd told off that tour bus driver named Bill. Now she wasn't angry, though. Now she just looked worried.

Worried and…kind. He thought, *She's good. A good woman. I could use a good woman in my life.*

Whatever his life was…

A hell of a mess he was in here, on his back in a blizzard, without a name, without any idea of who he was or where he'd come from, dressed for a much warmer place than the Sierras in a snowstorm.

She touched him, laying her mittened hand on the side of his face. He felt the warmth of her through the wool. "I'm sorry…"

He frowned at her. "Sorry?"

"For threatening you with that platter."

"Oh, that. 'S nothing."

"I should have seen you were hurt. But you came out of nowhere…"

"Didn't mean…scare you…" His lips felt strange and thick. They didn't want to talk.

"I'll call and get help." She started to rise.

He grabbed her arm to hold her with him. "No. Stay."

"You need a doctor."

"Stay."

She sighed and touched his face again. "Oh, you poor thing."

"I look…bad, huh?"

Her soft eyes, gold-flecked green, grew softer still. She asked in a gentle whisper, "What's happened to you?"

"I wish I knew," he heard himself mutter, with effort. "Tell me. Your…name?" His tongue wasn't working any better than his lips. Each word took form with tremendous difficulty.

"Tessa. Tessa Jones."

He repeated, "Tessa. Nice. Like it…"

The woman said something else. But he didn't hear her. He shut his eyes and let the strange white world and the big, kind-eyed clean-smelling woman drift away from him.

Chapter Two

The stranger's strong grip on Tessa's arm loosened and then dropped away.

A low cry of distress escaped her. Oh dear Lord, was he dead?

She ripped off a mitten and touched the side of his throat. The skin was cool beneath her fingers. His face had a grayish cast. But there *was* a pulse. She felt it beating, steady and true, against the pads of her first and middle fingers. And when she bent her head so her cheek was near his mouth, she felt his breath. Slow. Warm.

Alive.

His breath was sweet. But his jacket reeked of alcohol. Strange. But not the issue.

Help. Getting the man help. *That* was the issue.

She jumped to her feet. Thick snow whirled around her. She longed for a cell phone. But she rarely carried hers with her in town. No point in it. In North Magdalene, the mountains messed with the signals and a cell worked intermittently, at best.

She stared down at the man again. It seemed wrong to leave him alone in the snow, but what else could she do? Try and move him to the warmth of the house?

No. They always said it wasn't safe to move the badly injured, that you should wait for the EMTs.

Swiftly, she struggled out of her heavy jacket. Kneeling again, she settled it over the top of him, tucking it close. "I promise," she whispered, smoothing his snow-dusted black hair off his forehead, careful not to touch the angry-looking gash there. "I'll be right back...."

Again, she jumped up. That time, she made for the house, racing as fast as she could through the deepening snow. Inside, Mona Lou, her aging, deaf bulldog, and Gigi, her skinny, white, shorthaired cat, were sitting side by side in the front hall.

"Woof," said Mona Lou.

"Reow?" asked Gigi.

She dodged around them, headed for the wall phone in the kitchen, pulling off her mittens as she went.

Silence greeted her when she put the phone to her ear. She jiggled the hook. Nothing. A snow-laden tree branch had probably taken down a line somewhere. And judging by the look of the storm out there, the PG&E crews would be a while getting to it. She couldn't count on it coming back on any time soon.

What now?

She hustled to her bedroom, her dog and cat at her heels, and grabbed the cell she'd left by the bed. She tried 9-1-1. Nothing happened, except a pair of short beeps a few seconds later that meant the call had been dropped before it ever connected. She tried again.

No good. So all right. She would have to move the unconscious stranger herself, after all. Somehow.

And quickly. The snow was coming down so fast and thick now, it was going to be hard to see two feet in front of her face out there. At least her Subaru wagon had all-wheel drive. She would have to get the stranger into it and take him to the clinic herself.

Somehow…

Sled, she thought. She had a small one, a gift from her dad years and years ago, propped up on the enclosed front porch. She put her mittens back on, whispered, "Wish me luck," to Mona Lou and Gigi, and grabbed another jacket. She got a wool blanket from the closet and snatched her car keys from the key rack in the kitchen. As ready to face the near-impossible challenge as she was likely to get, she rushed back out the way she had come, only pausing to command Mona Lou, "Stay."

The dog couldn't hear much, but she picked up expressions and body language. She dropped to her haunches with a disgruntled whine.

On the porch, Tessa grabbed the sled and hoisted it under her free arm. The porch door bumped shut behind her as she emerged into the storm.

Lucky she'd put her purple coat on the man. The wind was blowing so hard, the heavy-falling snow swirling and eddying. She would have had to spend several precious minutes walking in circles until she stumbled on him—if not for the bright purple quilted fabric wrapped around his chest.

Muttering unheard apologies for moving him, she

managed to hoist his head and torso onto the too-short wooden slats. She tucked the coat around him tighter and wrapped the blanket around the coat and under his legs. He didn't look comfortable, not in the least. His poor head was canted at an odd angle on the red steering bar, his legs and feet dragging in the snow.

But it couldn't be helped. She couldn't carry him—she was strong, yes. But not *that* strong. What there was of the sled would have to do most of the work. Pausing only to check one more time and make sure he was still breathing—he was, thank the Lord—she looped the sled's towrope over her shoulder and hauled him, with considerable effort, toward the Subaru, which was parked in her driveway not far from the house.

How she did it, she hardly knew. But grunting and puffing, she dragged the man's limp body to the door behind the driver's seat. She even managed, by bracing herself in the open door and getting him firmly beneath her arms, to hoist him up across the backseat. Then she threw open the other door, wedged herself at the end of the seat, and dragged him the rest of the way inside. Finally, she raised his knees enough to get his boots clear of the door, tucked the coat and blanket around him again and shut both doors on his still form.

Panting, starting to sweat in spite of the frigid wind, she got behind the wheel and turned on the engine. Switching the heater on high, she aimed the defrost jets at the frozen, snow-thick windshield, which wouldn't be clearing any time soon unless she gave it a hand.

With a low moan of impatience and frustration, she found her scraper in the console, got out and scraped at the icy snow frozen to the glass, aware the whole time that precious seconds were ticking past and the stranger needed aid immediately. When she had the glass mostly cleared, she climbed behind the wheel again, shifted to reverse and backed the wagon toward the snow-covered road.

Luck was with her. She got turned around and pointed in the right direction, even got onto the road. But the snow was coming down so hard and so fast, she could hardly see, even with her wipers going full speed—which they weren't, since the snow had piled up so swiftly on the windshield, her wipers were laboring almost from the start. She saw that the snow would stop them. So she put it in park, got out and tried again to clean the snow out of the way.

Behind the wheel once more, she forged ahead. But the wipers were laboring again almost immediately, even though she had the defroster going full blast. The snow was just too much. She'd never seen such a storm.

Then the wipers stopped.

She turned them off, and then started them again. They made half an arc of the windshield, scratching ice, dragging snow, and then quit. So again, she turned them off. She stopped the wagon, got out, and again went through the process of brushing as much of the snow free of the wipers and windshield as she could.

When she got back behind the wheel, she tried them again. They worked. For a minute or two. But it was no good. No wipers in the world could keep up with the sheer volume of the white stuff tumbling down from above.

She tried leaning her head out the side window and driving that way. But the whirling snow made it almost impossible to see more than a few feet in front of her nose.

It wasn't going to happen. She didn't dare go on.

Moaning in distress for the unconscious man on the seat behind her, she put the Subaru in Reverse and backed it the way she had come. It was rough going, agonizingly slow.

But she made it at last, sliding into the parking space, right where she'd started, only pointed the opposite way. "Oh, I'm sorry," she told the man in back, as if he could hear her. "I'm so sorry. It was just too dangerous to go on."

Tessa put her head down on the steering wheel and let out a low moan—of fear for the stranger, of hopeless frustration. But no sooner had that moan escaped her than she drew herself up.

She was a Jones. She came from hardy, determined stock. A Jones man was the toughest, orneriest, un-beatable-est guy around. And a Jones woman? She was tougher still—after all, a Jones woman spent most of her life standing up to Jones men.

The man in the back seat needed warmth and shelter and a soft place to rest, at the very least. Tessa could do that much for him.

And she would.

Chapter Three

Warmth.

Impossible, but somehow, he was warm again. He moaned and opened his eyes. A ceiling. He was in a room. In a bed, his head on a white pillow, his body covered in a clean-smelling sheet and thick blankets. There was a dresser against the wall and a rocking chair in the corner. A shut door—to the closet or a bathroom?—on one side of the dresser, and an open one to a hallway on the other.

Gray daylight shone weakly in the wide window to the right of the bed. It was snowing hard, the white flakes hurling themselves at the glass.

A clock on the nightstand said it was 4:15 p.m. Vaguely, he recalled passing out in the snow. It had been sometime after noon then, hadn't it? That would mean he'd been out for at least a few hours. That is, if it was still the same day.

He looked around some more. There were lots of

framed photographs on the wall and on the dresser beside the dark eye of a small TV. They were, for the most part, pictures of a lot of people he'd never seen before.

But he did recognize the big blonde, the one who threw dishes and yelled at a guy named Bill. She was in several of the pictures. Laughing, with her head thrown back in one. Smiling broadly in another. And shyly in a third.

I'm in a bedroom in the blonde's house. He remembered the house—the tin roof, the chimney pipe with its trail of smoke spiraling into the gray sky....

When he'd passed out cold in the snow, the blonde must have brought him in here. Somehow. Or maybe someone else was here, someone who'd come out of the house after he was unconscious, someone who had helped her.

His mouth was dry as a desert ravine. He needed water. There was a white pitcher and an empty glass on the nightstand. He reached out his hand to the pitcher—and then let it drop. He'd have the pitcher's contents all over him if he tried to fill the glass lying down.

Okay, then. He would sit up.

With a groan, he popped to a sitting position. His head spun. So he dropped back flat again.

After a moment, he dragged himself up more carefully. That time, he managed to stay sitting until the spinning slowed a little. About then, he realized that beyond a wide variety of bruises and welts, his torso was bare. He pushed away the warm blankets.

She had taken his pants, too, leaving him in his boxers—black ones. Of silk, it appeared. Or was that satin? He felt a pained smile curve his lips as he realized that he didn't even recognize his own underwear.

The smile faded to a scowl as he continued the inventory of his battered body. His bare feet and legs were crisscrossed with strange, violent-looking bruises. She'd bandaged his cut-up knees.

He touched his face, felt gauze over the cut on the left side of his forehead. Weakness claimed him and he knew he didn't have the energy required to reach over, lift the pitcher and fill the glass.

Pitiful. Just pitiful. Wincing, flopping back down onto the pillow and dragging the blankets over himself again, he looked around the bedroom for his clothes and his shoes.

If they were there, he couldn't see them.

From somewhere in another part of the house, he heard conversation. A low drone of voices. At first he thought the blonde must be talking to someone, maybe whoever had helped her get him inside and into this bed—but then he heard music, a vaguely familiar commercial jingle, and he figured it out: Someone was watching TV.

He considered simply lying there until he felt up to trying to drink water again, to getting on his feet. Or until someone entered the room and saw he was awake. But in the end, he needed to know if the blonde was there, to be certain he wasn't alone in a strange house, with a TV left on in the other room.

"Hello?" It came out a raspy whisper. As if his voice had stopped working with the rest of him. He cleared his throat and tried again. "Hello?"

A moment later, she appeared, tall and strong and so healthy-looking, in the doorway. She wore a yellow sweater and blue jeans and a shining, hopeful smile. Her blond hair fell, thick and loose, on her shoulders.

There was a dog, too. A bandy-legged bulldog with a

patch over one eye. When she stopped in the doorway, the dog lumbered around in front of her and sat at her feet.

"You're awake!" She sounded absolutely thrilled.

Her excitement at his merely being conscious had the strangest effect on him. It warmed him within. He made his lips form a smile to answer hers.

"Water?" He croaked the word. "I can't…manage it."

She came to him and sat on the edge of the bed. He watched as she filled the glass from the pitcher. Gently, she slid a cool hand behind his head, lifting him enough that he could sip, and then putting the glass to his lips with care. "Easy," she whispered. "Take it slow…" The water moistened his dry mouth and soothed his parched throat.

"More," he croaked, when she took the glass away.

"Careful, okay? Not too much, not at first." She tipped the glass to his mouth again and he drank—less than he wanted. But enough that he no longer felt so dry.

She lowered his head back to the pillow and smoothed the covers around him. "Better?"

He breathed in that special, clean scent of hers. "Thank you."

"Give it a few minutes, to see if it stays down. Then if you want more—"

"Wait. No…"

She tipped her head to the side and the soft waves of her hair swung out. He wanted to touch those curls. They seemed so…vibrant. So full of that special warmth and goodness he had already come to associate with her. Her smile had changed, became a little puzzled. "No?"

"I mean, I'm not only thanking you for the water. Thank you for…everything. For saving me. Before I saw you, I was starting to think I would die."

She did what she'd done out in the snow, pressed her hand to the side of his face. It felt good there. "You did scare me, I have to admit. I thought more than once that I'd lost you. But here you are. Safe. Warm. And conscious. And that's just…" Her soft mouth bloomed into another sweet smile. "Terrific."

He remembered the trucker, his offer of a doctor, and realized he'd been pretty out of it, refusing medical care that way. "I guess you called a doctor, huh?"

She swallowed, glanced away.

He untangled an arm from under the covers and touched her—a brushing touch, on the side of her arm. "What? Is something wrong?"

She looked at him again. He did like her eyes, that light hazel color, green rayed with gold. Between her smooth brows there was a slight frown.

"Just tell me," he said. "Whatever it is, it can't be that bad."

She shrugged. "Well, that depends on what you call bad." A quivery sigh escaped her. "The phone's dead. And the snow is really coming down. It's just the two of us here and we're not getting out for a day or two, at least. Nobody's getting in, either. Including a doctor."

He took her hand then, and twined their fingers together. Strange, but it seemed the most natural thing, to hold her hand. She thought so, too—at least, she didn't try to pull away. He asked, "You've got plenty of wood for the fire, right?"

She nodded. "And propane heat, too. The tank out back is full, which is great."

"And food."

"That's right."

"And water and electricity. I even heard a TV."

"Yep. Everything's working fine. Except the phone."

"Tessa—it *is* Tessa, right?"

"Yep."

"Tessa," he said again, because he liked the sound of it. "I'll be okay now. I'm sure I will."

"Yes." She said it in a passionate whisper. "You'll be fine. Of course you will. Fine…" With the hand not captured in his, she touched his forehead, on the side without the bandage, in the tender, protective way his mother used to do when he was small.

His mother. He frowned. For a moment, in his mind's eye, he'd almost seen her face. But the image was gone in an instant. And his head was aching again. Not the ice-pick-stabbing ache, but the low, insistent throb.

"What is it?" Tessa leaned closer. "What's wrong?"

He squeezed her hand. "Headache."

"I can give you a mild painkiller—acetaminophen."

The way she said it made him smile. "You *can?*"

"Just now, before you called for me, I got out my trusty *Family Medical Guide* and did a little reading on traumatic brain injury."

Traumatic brain injury. It didn't sound good. "That's what I've got?"

"I'm no doctor, but it looks that way to me."

"And?"

"It's a myth that you can't have Tylenol. And you know how they always say don't let patients with head injuries sleep? That's a myth, too. You can sleep as much as you want."

"Good to know. What else?"

Something happened in those green-gold eyes. He suspected that a lot of what she'd read hadn't been especially reassuring. "Long story," she answered at last. "You can read it all yourself. Later." She pulled open the drawer in the nightstand and took out a bottle of Tylenol. Once she'd given him two and helped him swallow more water to wash them down, she tucked the covers up beneath his chin. "Rest a little. I'll be back to check on you every fifteen minutes or so. And if you need me, just give a holler."

"Will do."

She rose and started to go.

He stopped her in the doorway, where the bulldog waited. "One more thing…"

She turned back, her hand on the doorframe. "Yeah?"

"What did you do with my clothes?"

She made a sound in her throat. "Yikes. I guess that was kind of a shock, huh? Waking up in your underwear?"

"I got through it. And the whole process was a lot easier for me than for you—I mean, since I was out cold at the time and did nothing but just lie there."

She looked so earnest then. "I thought you'd be more comfortable, you know, without them. And then I did need to patch up your knees. That was easier without your pants in the way."

"Good call," he reassured her. "I just wondered where they were."

"They're laid out in the basement to dry now, but it's not looking real hopeful. Everything but the socks were dry clean only. I did what I could with them—mending them and cleaning them up, I mean. But most of those greasy black stains wouldn't come out."

"My boots?"

She folded her arms and leaned on the doorframe. "I put them near the woodstove in the other room—not too close, but close enough they'll dry a little faster."

"Thank you," he said, seriously now. "Again. For everything." They looked at each other across the short distance from the bed to the door. He liked looking at her.

She said, kind of shyly, "I have a question, too."

"Anything." He said it automatically, and then realized there were hundreds of questions—thousands—to which he had no answers. But he'd do his best.

For her.

"I don't know your name." She glanced downward, still shy. He thought how she'd managed to drag him in here, how she'd stripped him to his boxers and bandaged him up and put him in bed. How she'd mended his clothes and washed them and put his boots near—but not *too* near—the fire. All without even knowing his name.

Don't feel bad, he wanted to tell her. *I don't know my name, either.* But something had him holding back those words. He sensed that whoever he was in his real life, he wasn't a man who'd go around admitting that he had no clue who he was or where he'd come from. Uh-uh. Not even to the woman who had saved his life.

He smiled. Slowly. "You mean I failed to introduce myself?"

"As a matter of fact, you did."

"Bill," he said. "My name is Bill."

She laughed then, softly, leaning into the doorframe, that patch-eyed dog looking up at her. Then she drew herself up to her full six feet or so. "Oh, come on."

But he only insisted, "Call me Bill." Why not? It was as good a name as any. Maybe he'd be a better Bill than the idiot who'd jilted her for that showgirl. "Did you leave the rest of those dishes out there in the storm?"

She hitched up her chin. "You bet I did. They're buried already, not to be seen until the spring thaw."

"You've got quite an arm on you."

"I played basketball in high school. Shooting guard. Varsity team. *Boys'* varsity team." She spoke with pride. "It's a small school. They need every good shooting arm they can get."

"Wow. Impressive."

A modest nod. Then, firmly, "Rest."

"Rest, *Bill,*" he corrected.

"All right. Have it your way." Softly, she repeated, "Rest, *Bill.*"

He did rest. When he woke again, his headache had faded away and it was dark in the room. The curtains were drawn over the windows and no light bled in from outside. It must be nighttime.

The door to the hall was open. There was a light on, low, out there. The clock on the nightstand said it was 5:46 p.m. He started to call for Tessa, but then thought he'd try sitting up by himself again first.

His sore stomach muscles complained, but he did it. He reached for the switch on the bedside lamp and turned it on. Then he twisted to bolster the pillows against the headboard for support, and winced at the sharp pain down low on his belly.

What the hell? Wasn't there any part of his body that hadn't been bruised or bloodied?

He pushed back the blankets, eased the elastic of the boxers wide and peered inside. Good news: The family jewels were there, intact. But a deep bruise had imprinted itself in purple, green and black, across his lap. From some kind of belt restraint, maybe?

Car accident?

Was that it? He'd been in a car crash?

He studied his torso, checking for the mark of a chest restraint among all the other bruises. There wasn't one. Just a rainbow of black and purple splotches at random intervals on his ribcage and across his upper belly.

His head had started to pound again. He shut his eyes, breathed in and out through his nose. It worked. Slowly, the pounding faded. With a sigh of relief, he leaned back against the pillows. A minute or two ticked by as he gathered his strength for the next effort.

When he thought he could manage it, he tried for water—and succeeded. He reached over and poured some into the glass and brought the glass to his lips. It tasted like heaven, cool and refreshing. He was careful, as Tessa had warned him to be, not to gulp it down. He savored it—one swallow. Two.

So far, so good. He set the glass on his chest and rested again. Then he took a third sip.

"You *are* feeling better." She stood in the doorway, beaming.

He felt absurdly proud and raised the glass to her in a toast. "Yes, I am."

"I heated up some chicken broth. Think you're ready for that?"

He reached over and set the glass on the nightstand. "Bring it on."

She fed him the broth. Yeah, okay, he probably could

have managed to feed himself by then. But it felt good, to be spoiled by her. So he shamelessly accepted each salty, hot spoonful from her tender hands.

After that, she told him to rest again. He didn't argue. Obediently, he stretched out and let her smooth the covers over him. She turned off the light before she went out.

But the minute she left the room, he realized he needed a trip to the john. He considered calling her back.

But come on. Hadn't she done more than enough already? He could certainly deal with taking a whiz on his own. So he sat up, flipped the light back on and pushed back the covers. He swung his battered legs over the side of the bed. And then, one hand on the nightstand for balance, he pushed himself upright.

Not bad. Not bad at all.

Eyeing the shut door in the corner, he gauged the odds it would lead to a bathroom. Might as well find out. He started moving. It wasn't pretty. He shuffled along like a crippled old man. But at least he was on his feet and moving forward.

When he reached the door at last, he pulled it open on a combination closet and bath. The closet consisted of a recessed space to the left. Straight ahead was the bathroom. He hobbled on in there and took care of business.

After that, he washed his hands, taking his time over it as he stared at the stranger in the mirror. Black hair, blue eyes. A groove in his chin—what they called a cleft. A bandage covering the gash on his forehead. Bruises and scrapes everywhere…

There were lotions and creams on the sink counter. He picked up one of the bottles and read the tiny print on the back, which taught him not only that the lotion contained glycerin and almond oil, but also that his eyesight was pretty damn good.

Whoever he was, he probably didn't need glasses.

Once he'd dried his hands and hung the hand towel back on its hook, he snooped around some more.

One drawer held makeup in trays, another brushes and combs. A third, a blow-dryer and one of those curling-iron things.

Taking it slow, he returned to the bedroom.

She was waiting for him. "I thought I heard the toilet flush…" She started toward him. "Here. Let me—"

He put up a hand. "Tessa."

"Hmm?"

"Leave a man a little damn dignity, will you?"

She stopped in midstep. "Have it your way…Bill." She turned her back, giving him at least a show of privacy, as he shuffled his way to the bed, got in and arranged the covers over himself.

"This is your room, isn't it?" he asked when he was settled.

She faced him with a nod. "I have a spare sleeping area, but it's a loft. No way was I dragging you up the stairs. Not good for you, way too much work for me."

"I'm sorry to put you out of your room."

"Couldn't be helped. And if you want to show you're really grateful, get well."

"I'm working on it."

"You do seem better."

"I am. Is there a remote for the TV?"

"In the nightstand drawer." She was leaning in the doorway again.

He opened the drawer and took out the remote and

pointed it at the TV, which came on to a commercial of a woman in an evening dress mopping a kitchen floor. "Local news?"

She told him the channel. He switched to it and got the weather report. A sexy brunette stood in front of a Doppler-radar map of the western states. "This is a bad one, folks. A blizzard for the record books. The front is slow-moving, which means it will be hanging around over the northern Sierra, dumping up to eight feet of snow before it's over…"

Tessa said, "Funny about the weather report. Half the time it's nothing you couldn't learn by looking out the window." And she left him.

He sipped more water and waited for the rest of the news, which came after the weather, the blizzard being the main event.

The second story had him sitting up straighter: a Learjet had crashed in nearby Plumas County, in a snowy field not far from the intersection of Highway 49 and Gold Lake Road. The business jet, owned by a Texas-based company called BravoCorp, had been en route to the Bay Area, and blown off course by the storm.

He was reasonably certain the highway that went through North Magdalene was Highway 49. Although he couldn't recall when or how the trucker had picked him up, he remembered the ride. More or less. There had been a sign, hadn't there, one that said it was Scenic Highway 49?

His heart pounded faster to match the ache in his head as he waited for a picture of the face he'd seen in the bathroom mirror to flash on the screen, to hear his real name, and that they were looking for him.

But then the pretty, sincere-sounding newscaster said

the pilot, copilot and single passenger had miraculously all survived the crash and were hospitalized in fair-to-critical condition...

All present and accounted for. His pulse stopped galloping and the throb in his head diminished. If he'd been in a crash, it hadn't been on that particular plane.

The news continued. No stories of car crashes or men in clothing inappropriate for freezing weather going missing somewhere in the Sierras. If anyone was looking for him, they hadn't managed to get it on the news.

He flipped channels for a while. There weren't many of them. Eventually, he gave up and turned it off. He put the remote on the nightstand and dozed.

After the stranger in her bedroom managed to make it to the bathroom on his own, Tessa decided that checking on him every fifteen minutes was probably overkill. She looked in on him at 7:00 p.m. and again at 7:30. That second time, after he'd been asleep for a while, she crept in to turn off the light and ended up standing by the bed, gazing down at him. He seemed to be sleeping peacefully.

In the light that bled in from the hallway, she studied his face. It was a very handsome face, square-jawed, with a cleft in the chin and a blade of a nose. His mouth had a certain sexy, tempting curve to it. His hair was black as night and thick, the kind of hair any normal woman would want to run her fingers through. The white bandage on his forehead stood out against his tanned skin. He needed a shave. But the shadow of beard on his sculpted cheekbones only made him look more handsome. More masculine...

Bill, he'd called himself. She felt her lips curve in a

smile at the thought. The man was a whole other kind of Bill from the one who had dumped her for a showgirl.

She turned off the light and tiptoed out the door, where Mona Lou was waiting for her, looking slightly puzzled as to why there was a strange man in her human's bed. Tessa knelt and gave the dog a scratch right where she liked it, in the folds of her neck. She pressed her cheek to Mona's warm, short coat and whispered, "Don't worry, everything's fine."

The dog let out a low whine and wagged her stumpy tail in response.

In the kitchen, Tessa dished up wet food for both Mona Lou and Gigi. Then she made herself a sandwich and ate in the great room with the TV on, changing the channels, looking for a news bulletin about a tall, blue-eyed, black-haired man who'd gone missing in the Sierras wearing light-weight slacks, a buff-colored jacket and a cashmere sweater.

There was no bulletin. She cleaned up after her meal and went back to her chair in front of the TV. With Gigi cuddled up beside her and Mona stretched out at her feet, she switched channels some more, looking for news of the stranger. She wished she had the Internet—her service was dial-up, no good with the phone dead. Only last summer, North Magdalene had gotten broadband service. She should have switched over, but somehow she'd never gotten around to it.

After checking on her patient again and finding him sleeping, she tried to read. It was hard to concentrate. She was worried about him.

He seemed to be doing pretty well—clear-headed when awake and enjoying normal sleep. But he'd been comatose for hours in the afternoon. According to her *Family*

Medical Guide, extended unconsciousness after head trauma was not a good thing. The book advised calling an ambulance when a head trauma victim passed out. He might have a subdural hematoma, blood on the brain. And if he did have one of those and it was acute, even with treatment, which he was *not* getting, he could die.

The book also said that, as she'd suspected, she shouln't have moved him. She should have covered him and made him as comfortable as possible where he was and then waited for professional help. Too bad the book didn't say what to do when you were stuck in a blizzard with the phone line down.

The phone. Maybe it had come on again.

She checked. Still dead.

He's fine, she kept telling herself. *He's going to be fine.*

And then she would stew over how he'd told her nothing about himself except that she should call him Bill. He hadn't mentioned who might be worried for him, who might be wondering where he'd gone off to and if he was okay.

She had a feeling he didn't know who he was.

Amnesia. It was one of the symptoms—along with headache, unconsciousness and mental confusion—of acute subdural hematoma. *Amnesia.* She reached for the medical guide again and looked up the scary word. The book said there were several different types of memory loss. It could happen from emotional trauma. Or head trauma—which it was obvious he'd had.

Then again, maybe he knew exactly who he was. Maybe he was just a closed-mouth kind of guy. Or maybe he had done something…bad. Something he was keeping—along with his identity—strictly to himself.

Maybe he had some other totally valid reason to keep

who he really was a secret. She just couldn't believe he had evil intent. He seemed a good man.

Didn't he?

How could she tell? How could she know?

Look at Bill Toomey. Tessa groaned and shook her head. The tour bus driver had not been her first romantic disappointment. She had to admit that she wasn't any great judge of male character. The Bill in her bedroom could be a bad man. Or a good one. He could be hiding something—or simply have forgotten who the heck he was.

Wait, she thought. *Why think the worst?* The man in her bedroom had been grateful and respectful. And polite. He'd done nothing to make her think ill of him. Until he did something out of line, she would believe in his basic decency and leave it at that.

She went in to check on him at 10:20. He was sleeping peacefully. She took her cell out with her when she left the room.

In the great room, she dialed her dad's number. Nothing. Feeling slightly frantic, she tried the kitchen phone again. Silence.

She was alone with the stranger and she'd better get used to it. There was no need to panic. He was going to get well. After all, he *had* been sleeping normally when she checked on him—or at least, she thought he had.

No. Think positive. She *knew* he had. He was getting better. She was certain of that.

He started shouting at 10:45 p.m.

Chapter Four

A woman was screaming. *"Ohmigod, ohmigod, we're going to die! I can't die. Somebody help me! Help me, Ash. Help me, please!"*

Then a man's voice shouted, "Sit still! Be calm!"

The shouting startled him to wakefulness. Only then did he realize that the shouting had come from his own mouth. "Wha...?"

A tall figure appeared in the doorway. He saw broad, shapely shoulders, a halo of golden hair. Was this the one who had screamed?

No. The screaming had only been inside his mind.

And then he remembered: This was the woman who had saved him....

He lifted his head, straining, off the sweat-drenched pillow, and whispered her name on a rough husk of breath, "Tessa," as she came to him.

"It's okay, it's okay," she promised in a gentle whisper.

He felt her cool hand on his sweaty brow, drank in her soothing voice. It wasn't enough. He came up off the pillow again and grabbed for her, needing the feel of her, the living reality of her.

The warmth.

The softness and the strength. He wrapped his arms hard around her, buried his face against her sweet-smelling throat.

She didn't resist him, didn't try to pull away. She only stroked his back and let him hold her way too tight and whispered, again, "Okay. It's okay…."

He was breathing like he'd just run a damn marathon, his sore ribs aching as he gulped in air. The sweat poured off him.

"You're okay. You're safe," she whispered. "You're here. In my house. Safe…" In spite of his powerful grip on her, she managed to reach out and turn on the lamp.

Still struggling to catch his breath, he blinked against the sudden brightness. But then, in no time, his breathing began to even out and his eyes adjusted to the light. He shifted his hold to her sweet face and cradled it between his palms. He stared hard into her beautiful eyes.

"It's okay," she promised him, meeting his gaze without wavering, seeming to will him to trust her. To believe. "It's all right. All right…"

Slowly, he came back to himself—whoever that self was. He released her. "Sorry. Didn't mean to grab you. So damn sorry…"

She only plumped the pillows against the headboard for him. And then she poured him fresh water from the pitcher. He drank. She took the glass when he was finished and set it back on the nightstand.

"Better?"

He nodded. "I was dreaming. It was a nightmare, that's all."

"A nightmare about…?"

He tried to remember, but it was pointless. "I have no idea. I heard a woman screaming. And then someone shouting. It woke me up, the shouting. Then I realized the shouting was coming from me."

"What else?"

"Nothing. That's it. That's…all."

She asked, so gently, "Who are you, really?"

Her question was the toughest one, the one that brought pain. He waited for the ice pick to go to work on his brain. But there was nothing. Only emptiness.

His own life was lost to him. He wished he had an answer for her. And for himself.

She prompted, "Do you *know* who you are?"

He opened his mouth to lie, to remind her that his name was Bill and yeah, damn right he knew who he was. But then he realized he couldn't do it. It seemed…wrong, somehow. Disrespectful. To keep on trying to hide the truth from her. If not for her, he'd be curled up in a snowbank somewhere. Dead.

He confessed, "I have no clue who I am. Or where I came from."

She made a low sound of sympathetic distress, a world of kindness and understanding shining in her eyes. "I'm so sorry."

"Don't be. You, of all people, have nothing to be sorry about." He clasped her shoulder, thinking again how much he liked touching her. "Bill, okay? I'm serious. Let me be Bill. I'll be a better Bill than that other fool. I swear it. I would never leave you at the altar."

She frowned, clearly confused. "The altar? Bill Toomey didn't leave me at the altar."

Maybe it hurt her too much to admit it. He back-pedaled. "Well. Okay. I must have, er, misunderstood."

"Misunderstood what?"

"Tessa. It doesn't matter."

"Well, yeah. It does. I want to know where you got the idea that Bill and I were engaged."

"Out in the snow. When you were breaking the dishes? You talked about 'the wedding,' how Bill had promised you he'd be there for the wedding."

A low laugh escaped her. "Oh, that."

"Yeah," he said gruffly. "That."

"I meant the wedding of a friend of mine. Bill promised he'd come to town for it. It's Saturday, the twenty-sixth, two weeks from today."

"Saturday." So strange. Not even to know what day it was. "It's Saturday, today?"

"That's right. Saturday the twelfth."

"Of?"

She gave him one of those looks of hers—a look of sweet and tender understanding. "January."

"Well, all right. And so your friend's having herself a winter wedding?"

"Uh-huh. Tawny—Tawny Riggins, my friend and my second cousin by marriage—always wanted a January wedding, even though everyone kept telling her she was crazy, that bad weather could ruin it. But Parker Mont-gomery, her fiancé, who also happens to be a second cousin by marriage, only a *different* marriage…" Her voice trailed off. She slanted him a look. "Sorry."

"What for?"

"More information than you could possibly have needed or wanted."

"Did I say that?"

She shrugged. "No. You were being polite."

"Not so. I'm hanging on every word."

She laughed. "Oh, I'll bet."

"Honest truth."

"It's only…small towns, you know. Everybody's related to everyone else. Anyway, it'll be a winter wedding and Bill said he would be my date for it."

"So it's not as bad as I thought, then."

"What isn't?"

"The idiot didn't jilt you."

"No. He only dumped me. But I broke half the dishes he gave me. That really helped me put things in perspective. I'm so over him." She laughed. "All of a sudden, I can't even remember his name."

"Wait a minute. The fool gave you…dishes?"

"Oh, yeah. FestiveWare, it's called. It comes in all these great colors, used to be popular back in the nineteen-twenties and thirties. They started making it again in the nineties. I told him I always wanted a place setting in every color. So he bought them for me. I was thrilled at the time. That was when our love was new, you might say."

"Back when you could still remember his name, you mean?"

"That's right, during the first week we spent together, when I went to Napa to tour the wine country last summer."

"And Bill drove the tour bus…."

"I've gotta say. Your memory is certainly crystal clear on the subject of…what was his name again?"

He grinned. "You, in the snow, throwing dishes. *That,* I'll always remember. Every plate you threw, every word you said."

"Great." She sounded resigned.

"Tell me the rest."

"The rest of what?"

"Well, how did you find out about the showgirl?"

"Seriously, you do not need to know."

"I do," he insisted. "Tell me."

"You should be resting."

"Tell me."

"Oh, fine." She wrinkled her nose. "A letter. He broke up with me in a letter. I suppose I should count my blessings. At least he didn't do it by e-mail."

"You got the letter today, then?"

She nodded. "I heard the storm was coming in, so I closed up my store—I own a shop on Main Street—and I picked up my mail at the post office and I came home. I'd seen the letter in the stack and I was all excited, looking forward to hearing from him-whose-name-I-can't-recall. I sat at my kitchen table and put the bills and junk mail aside. And read the letter. After I read it, I burned it. Then I got the dishes he gave me and lugged them out into the snow…and the rest, you know. I suppose you might say I kind of lost it, went a little crazy, when I read that letter."

"A *little?*"

"Okay. It was more than a little. I went crazy…a lot."

"Luckily, though, you're past all that now."

"I am. It's a miracle. My broken heart is totally mended."

"So call me Bill. Take me to the wedding of Tawny and Parker. After all, you did tell everyone that I was coming…."

She laughed. And then she grew serious. Gently, she reminded him, "We just met. You're not well. And two weeks is…a long time from now."

He couldn't argue with that one. "Fair enough. For now, I'll be satisfied if you'll just call me Bill."

"Bill," she said. "All right. Bill." When she looked at him like that, he thought that being some guy named Bill wouldn't be half-bad. "Tell me," she coaxed, "I mean, if you feel up to it. Tell me what you *do* know. What you remember…about your life. About yourself."

"That'll be over nice and quick."

"I *would* like to know." The bulldog, which had been sitting in the doorway until then, lumbered over. Tessa bent and scratched its wrinkled head. "Unless you're too tired…"

He couldn't refuse her. "I'm okay. Really." She was, after all, his hero, the one who had saved him from certain death. "I remember riding in a big rig down Highway 49. That was today, some time before noon…" He shared what little he had to call memory—the ride into North Magdalene, the driver who tried to help him, the trek through town and along the highway to the tree-shaded road that led to her house. As he'd predicted, it took hardly any time to tell: the sum of his life, all he could recall of it, in a few sorry sentences. At the end, he shrugged. "The rest you know better than I do."

She laid her palm, as she had twice before, along the side of his face. "It will be okay. You'll see. It will all work out." She spoke fervently.

He put his hand over hers. "Whatever happened to me

before this, I finally got lucky. I found you." Okay, it sounded sappy as hell. But too bad. It was the truth.

Tessa gazed at him so tenderly—or she did until she seemed to catch herself. She pulled her hand away, sat back from him a little and cleared her throat. He knew she was striving for just the right words—words that wouldn't hurt his feelings, but would make it clear she wasn't interested in getting anything romantic going with him.

He changed the subject before she found a way to tell that lie. "Two things I want now. Don't say I can't have them."

"Well, that depends," she said, all brisk and business-like, "on what they are."

"Solid food."

A tight, careful smile. "I can do that."

"And even before food, I really need a shower—and don't give me that look."

"What look?"

"Doubtful. Worried. I can hack a shower."

"Your bandages…"

"A bath, then. I can be careful of my knees and my head. I mean, if you've got a tub…" The bathroom he'd used earlier only had a shower stall.

"There's a tub in the hall bath." She still looked unsure. But then she sighed. "I suppose if your bandages get wet, we can just change them."

"Exactly."

"And I've got some sweats that are a little too big for me. They might fit you, or close enough. And some wool socks left here by…never mind."

"You're blushing."

"I am not."

He teased, "I want to know all your secrets, Tessa Jones."

She made a humphing sound. "Only if you tell me yours."

"Too bad I don't have any—at least, none I can remember."

She gazed at him so intently. "It'll come back, your memory. In time. You'll see."

He liked her simple faith in positive outcomes. She made him think of those bumper stickers that commanded, *Expect a miracle.* Only she *was* the miracle.

"A bath," he said again. "Please."

"All right. If you really think you *have* to…"

She gave him a stack of stuff to take in there with him: the sweats, the socks, a toothbrush, toothpaste. "There are clean towels on the rack and shampoo and soap in the cabinet." She even offered one of her pink disposable razors and a can of feminine shaving cream. He took it all with a grateful smile.

Once the tub was full, he sank into it with a long sigh, careful to keep his bandaged knees above the water. He could have stayed in there forever, soaking his aches and pains away. But his stomach kept complaining. He needed food. So he washed and got out and shaved with the razor she'd given him, lathering with her shave cream that smelled like tropical flowers. He brushed his teeth and put on the sweats, which fit well enough, although given a choice, he would have gone for something that wasn't light purple. The socks—whoever they'd once belonged to—were thick and warm.

And the bandage on his forehead was coming loose. He pried it off the rest of the way and studied the injury in the medicine cabinet mirror. It wasn't pretty. It also wasn't bleeding anymore, so he figured he'd just go without a bandage for now.

In the kitchen, she told him he looked fabulous in lilac. She took his boxers to wash, disappearing downstairs to start a load. When she came back up, she checked the wound and agreed it was probably okay to leave it uncovered. She gave him half a roast beef sandwich. He wolfed it down and she passed him the other half. And an apple. And a tall glass of milk.

By then, he was tired again. But he was also enjoying himself. A lot. He was warm and his stomach was full. His headache seemed to have taken a break. Sitting there with her at her kitchen table…well, he couldn't think of anywhere else he would rather be.

True, he didn't have a lot to compare the moment to, given that he couldn't recall being very many places: the highway known as 49, the town called North Magdalene and this small, plain house of hers. They were his whole life, as of now. They were all he knew, all he'd ever known.

It was damn scary.

But when he looked across the table at her, all he could think was that he never would have met her—if whatever had happened to him *hadn't* happened. That seemed impossible, not to have met Tessa Jones. Impossible and wrong.

From where he sat, he could see most of her great room. The bulldog was asleep on a rag rug a few feet from the woodstove. There was a white cat on the sofa. An old-fashioned clock on the rough mantel over the stove chimed midnight, softly. He'd known her for almost twelve hours. It was forever. It was his whole life.

She left him to go down to the basement and move the load of laundry to the dryer.

"You're drooping in that chair," she said, when she came back up.

"Sit down."

She shook her head, but she did sit.

He asked, "What's the dog's name?"

"Mona Lou."

"And the cat?"

"Gigi."

"Tell me about your family."

"Bill, did you hear me? You should go back to bed."

"I will. In a while. Are your parents still alive?"

"Yes."

"Still married?"

She shook her head. "My mom lives in Arkansas. My dad's still here, in North Magdalene. He got married again when I was twelve, to Miss Regina Black. Gina was what they used to call a spinster in the old days. She was in her thirties when my dad swept her off her feet. They eloped to Reno. We were living in Arkansas then, but when my dad and Gina married, my mom let us come back home and live with them."

"Us?"

"I have a sister, Marnie. She's three years younger than me."

"Tall and blonde like you?"

"Not so tall. Brown hair. Completely different personality."

"Different, how?"

"Come on. I know you're tired…"

He didn't budge. "Uh-uh. I want to hear about your sister. How's she different from you?"

She gave him a long look of disapproval. But in the

end, she did answer his question. "Marnie was a crazy and wild little tomboy with a bad attitude when she was a kid."

"You were the good sister?"

"Too good."

"No."

"Yeah. Too good. Seriously. We were always fighting, back then, Marnie and me. But since we've grown up, we get along fine. She lives with her boyfriend, Mark, now. In Santa Barbara. Mark and Marnie have been best friends since they were kids. Mark's dad is Lucas Drury. He's a bestselling author. Writes horror stories? And Lucas is now married to my cousin, Heather. But Lucas had Mark by his first wife." She laughed. "Like I said before, it's a small town. A girl can't turn around without running into a relative."

He liked listening to her talk and he liked hearing about her family. "And you get along okay, then, with your stepmother?"

"Gina? I love her. We all love her. My dad was a mess before he got together with her. He was troubled and wild, like most of the men in my family. He drank too much and went out with a woman named Chloe Swan. Big trouble, that Chloe. Once she even shot him."

He laughed. "You're not serious."

"Oh, I am. She was trying to shoot Gina, actually. But my dad got in the way."

"He took a bullet for your stepmother?"

"Yeah. That's love for you, huh?"

"But he recovered?"

"Fully. And Chloe went to prison for a few years. Since she got out, she's had the good sense to leave my dad alone. Guess she finally figured out that Gina is the only woman for Patrick Jones. With Gina, my dad found out how to be happy. With Gina, we *all* found out how to be happy."

"Did they have more kids, together?"

"Gina and my dad? Oh, yeah. They had three more. My half-sister, Anthea, who's thirteen now, and two boys, Brady and Craig, nine and eight. They're my brothers and I love them, but they are holy terrors. Jones boys always are."

"Why do you say that?"

"You would have to know the Joneses."

"I *will* know the Joneses. As soon as it stops snowing. I think you should prepare me for that."

"I'd be happy to, tomorrow. But now, it's your bedtime."

He sat back in the chair. "Kind of bossy, aren't you, Tessa?"

"It's your health I'm thinking about." She pinched up her mouth at him.

He laughed. It felt good. Yeah, it made his head hurt. But so what? A good laugh was worth a little pain.

She looked more than a little annoyed with him. "Did I say something funny?"

He pushed back the chair and got to his feet. "You're cute. A cute woman."

Now she *was* annoyed. No doubt about it. She drew her strong shoulders back and aimed a thumb at her nicely rounded breasts. "I am five-foot-eleven and you should see me chop wood. I am not, nor have I ever been, cute."

"Cute," he repeated and came around the table toward her. "Just completely…cute."

When he reached her, he held down a hand. She looked at it, narrow-eyed, and then up at him. "What are you up to now?"

"Come on, take my hand."

"Bill…"

"Take it."

With a small, impatient huff of breath, she put her fingers in his. He pulled her upright.

She rose with easy grace. At her full height, they were almost eye to eye. He estimated he was maybe two inches taller than she was. He found he liked that. A woman who could drag a man out of a blizzard and into her house, get him undressed and bandaged up and into her bed. A resourceful woman. A woman of substance.

"The best kind," he whispered.

"What *are* you talking about?"

"You." He grasped her waist and pulled her just a little bit closer.

Her mouth quivered. She bit her lower lip to make it stop and put her hands on his shoulders to keep him at bay. Her body trembled slightly in his hold and that pleased him. "This is…a bad idea, Bill."

"What?" He tried to look as innocent as possible, given that he was not.

"I think that maybe *you're* thinking…of kissing me."

"You do, huh?"

"Well. Are you?"

He crinkled his brow, as if deep in thought.

"Are you?" she demanded, more strongly that time.

He smiled at her. Slowly. "As a matter of fact, I am."

Chapter Five

"Bill." She said his new name kind of breathlessly.

"That's me." He touched her chin. Smooth. Warm. Full of life. He traced the back of a finger down the side of her neck, just beneath the soft fall of her hair.

"I…um…" Her breathing was agitated. He could see in those beautiful eyes that she wanted him to kiss her, no matter what that mouth of hers was saying. "You shouldn't. Really."

"Yeah. I should."

"Bill, I don't…"

He took her mouth. Because he *had* to kiss her. And also to make her stop telling him not to. He gathered her in, wrapping his arms around her, pulling her close enough that her breasts pressed against his chest.

She sighed. Her body went pliant.

So he kissed her some more, deepening the contact,

pulling her into him, thoroughly enjoying the strong, sub-
stantial shape of her all along the front of him. She
allowed that, allowed him to press his body to hers. He
tasted the slick surfaces beyond her parted lips. Good. She
tasted so good....

Eventually, with considerable regret, he lifted his head.

She gazed at him through stricken eyes. "You shouln't
have done that."

He touched her chin again and idly stroked her soft
cheek. "Yeah. I should have. I want to do a lot more..."

"Bill. Please. We hardly know each other. And neither
of us needs this kind of trouble."

"Wrong. I do. I need it. I need it a lot."

"This is crazy."

He couldn't have agreed with her more. "Yeah. You're
right. It is. Crazy in a very good way."

She didn't look all that pleased. "Time for you to go
to bed. Alone."

He slipped his hand under the silky fall of her hair and
clasped the back of her neck. What a woman.

"Bill."

"Okay." He released her, stepping back. "Good
night, Tessa."

She blinked. "I...good night."

He turned and left her standing there.

Tessa watched him until he disappeared into the hallway
at the other end of the kitchen. She heard him quietly close
the bedroom door. Once she knew she was alone, that he
wasn't coming back, she lifted her hand and touched her
lips where the warmth of his kiss still lingered.

She sank back to her chair, feeling sucker-punched.

She couldn't believe she had done that, let him kiss her. Kissed him back.

It was…inappropriate. Beyond tacky, to have kissed him. He was in no condition to be kissing anyone— although she had to admit, for someone who didn't even know his own name, he sure knew what to do with those warm lips of his.

But what was she *thinking?* Until around noon that day, she'd been in love with Bill Toomey—hadn't she?

Uh, well, judging by how quickly and thoroughly she'd put him from her mind, apparently not. She felt…embarrassed, at how effortlessly she'd recovered from losing him, when she'd told everyone in town that she was certain, this time, she'd gotten it right. That this time, she'd found the guy for her.

Yeah. She was embarrassed, and a little ashamed.

Tessa knew what people in town said about her. And she hated being forced to admit that they were probably right. For a solid, dependable person who pulled her own weight in almost every aspect of her life, she was a total idiot when it came to love and romance.

Eventually, after sitting at the table alone for maybe fifteen minutes, calling herself all kinds of irresponsible fool, she rose and went upstairs to get the pajamas she'd taken from her own room earlier. She used the hall bath for a quick shower and to brush her teeth. After that, she turned off most of the lights on the lower floor, leaving one on low in the hallway, just in case. She turned down the heater and adjusted the damper on the stove. And then, at last, she climbed the stairs to her temporary bed, Mona and Gigi at her heels.

Under the covers, with Gigi at her feet and Mona

already making those sleepy snorking sounds beside her, Tessa called herself a fool again and tried to convince herself that she was going to be more wary of the stranger sleeping in her room.

Really, he was far from the type of guy she would normally look twice at. He was too handsome, too…smooth. Worst of all, there was an excess of testosterone going on with him. As a rule, she never went for the super-manly type. She liked men who were shy and sweet. Innocent, even—men nothing like the wild males in her family.

Yet, handsome, smooth and macho as he clearly was, the stranger named Bill *had* charmed her. He seemed honestly to like her—to admire her, even—and to be so grateful for the way she'd taken care of him.

But it could all be an act. He could murder her in her bed.

A low laugh bubbled up at the thought. She stifled it with a hand over her mouth. Just look at her. Laughing at the idea that the man downstairs might harm her. She needed to be more careful around him—and she would in the future.

However, she simply couldn't buy that he presented a physical danger to her. She just didn't believe it. She had this absolute certainty that if he was a threat to her, it was to her heart and not to her safety.

Tessa rubbed her eyes. All this stewing wasn't going to change a thing. She needed to put her doubts and fears aside and rest a little while she could. In an hour or two, she would be getting up and going down to check on him again. She set the clock by the bed for 3:00 a.m. And then she yawned, pulled the covers close and turned on her side.

Within minutes, she was deep in dreams.

* * *

In Tessa's bedroom, the man who called himself Bill was still awake. He'd taken off the purple sweats and the thick borrowed socks and climbed under the covers naked.

Propped against the pillows, he'd been channel-surfing. He flipped through the few available channels, staring blankly at the TV screen, telling himself he was looking for a news flash about someone fitting his description going missing, but not really paying a lot of attention to what he was watching.

For the most part, he kept his mind as blank as his stare. Straining to remember who he was and where he came from only made the headache start stabbing.

No. For now, he might as well accept that he was Bill. Bill, who had claimed a first kiss from Tessa Jones. The taste of her was on his tongue and the clean scent of her stayed with him, arousing to him. She had kept him alive. And now, she was giving him memories. Good memories. Sweet ones.

He wanted to kiss her some more. He wanted to take off all her clothes and touch her naked body everywhere. Making love to Tessa. Now, that would be a memory to treasure. Beneath the sheet, he felt himself hardening.

He raised the blankets and took a look. That particular piece of equipment was not only intact, but apparently working A-OK. Good to know. Too bad about his brain.

But a man can't have everything.

He stared at the TV a while longer, thinking about the family story Tessa had told him. She had two sisters and two brothers. And her dad loved his wife. It all sounded pretty good to him.

Did he have a family beyond the mother he'd vaguely

remembered—or imagined he remembered—earlier that day? Did he have a dad? Brothers and sisters?

In his head, the faint throbbing started. He shut his eyes, thought about nothing, until the throbbing went away.

Then he stared at the TV some more, his mind mostly occupied with thoughts of Tessa, of how, if he had to start his life all over again with a blank slate for a mind and nothing in his pockets, so be it. At least he'd had the good fortune to end up at the tender mercy of Tessa Jones.

He glanced at the clock. It was almost 2:00 a.m.

He shut off the television, turned out the light and stretched out on his back to wait for sleep. It was a long time coming. But eventually, the darkness behind his eyes faded and he dreamed.

In his dreams, he found his family. He walked the rooms of the big ranch house at Bravo Ridge, where he'd grown up. He stood in the grand entry hall and talked to his mother, Aleta, who kept changing, her face melting and re-forming into an older woman and then a younger one.

One minute, she was as he remembered her in his childhood, bluebonnet eyes shining, her skin soft, her slim hands smooth and veinless. But tired. She was always tired back then. With nine children in ten years, who wouldn't be?

And then she was herself, now, in her fifties, but still beautiful, her chestnut hair showing no gray.

"Ash," she said. "Are you sure this is what you want?"

"Of course." His voice was flat, without inflection.

"But will you be happy?"

Happy. As if that was the question. Still, he loved his mother and he told her what she wanted to hear. "You bet. I'm the happiest man alive."

Aleta shook her head. She looked so sad. He started to tell her not to worry, it was a hell of a match, good for everyone, and everything would be okay. But she was fading. He could see the far wall through her body. She disappeared.

The walls melted and reformed around him and he was in a board meeting, one that went on forever. Once all the arguments were made, his father spoke. His brother Gabe, an attorney, the family fixer, said he'd see what he could do.

The dreamer looked down and saw he held a small velvet jewelry box. He flipped the box open. A diamond engagement ring and a wedding ring to match. The enormous engagement diamond gleamed at him, blinding in its hard brightness.

"What do you think?" he asked, looking up.

Gabe said, "Are you kidding me? It's gorgeous. She'll love it."

The dreams of home faded. He forgot the names of the people in them. He forgot everything.

The world exploded and he was spinning, falling, down and down, the universe above him, clouds around him, the world somewhere below, rising to meet him, bringing the end of him…

And then, a soft hand on his forehead, a gentle voice whispering, "Shh. Shh, now…"

He freed an arm and grabbed the wrist of that hand in a punishing hold. He heard a gasp. And he opened his eyes. The lamp he'd switched off was on again. A woman loomed above him, her wrist in his grip. Blond hair. Eyes green and rayed with purest gold…

"Tessa." He released her.

She rubbed her wrist where his fingers had manacled it

and forced a trembling smile. "You're awake. And you know who I am." She let out a long breath of pure relief. "Good."

He was covered in sweat again, same as when he woke up from that other nightmare. He started to push back the covers, but remembered in time that he was naked. With a ragged sigh, he let his head drop back to the damp pillow.

She said, "I came down to check on you. You were moaning in your sleep, tossing your head from side to side, mumbling, '*No*,' over and over again."

"I…hurt you." He despised himself.

She dropped her arm to her side, her pajama sleeve falling over it, so he couldn't see her wrist. "It's nothing. Really."

"No. Let me see…"

"Bill. It's okay."

He reached out. "Let me see." He caught her gaze. Held it. "Come on…"

Reluctantly, she gave him her hand. He pushed back the flannel sleeve. The soft skin around her wrist was red where he'd grabbed her.

"It's fine," she insisted. "Truly."

"Tessa." He held her eyes again.

Her broad shoulders sagged. "What?"

He brought her wrist to his lips and he kissed the soft flesh where he'd hurt her. "I'm so sorry. I never want to hurt you."

"I know you don't. You haven't. Really. It's only a little redness. No big deal. It'll fade in a few minutes." Her voice was a trembling whisper. She opened her hand and caressed the side of his face the way she liked to do.

And he went on looking at her, with her gold hair sleep-tangled around her face, in cute red pajamas with little snowmen all over them. He couldn't get enough of looking at her. Her mouth was so pink and soft, it made him start to get hard again, just looking at it. He remembered the kiss before she'd sent him to bed. How could he ever forget that kiss?

He couldn't.

He wouldn't.

And he wanted another.

He reached up, slid his fingers around her neck, feeling that amazing silky hair falling over the back of his hand. "Tessa…"

"Oh," she said. "Oh, see, we shouldn't. We really…" Her protests trailed off into silence.

Good. He pulled her down, until her mouth touched his. She sighed, her lips parting. He breathed her in, tightening his hold a little, bringing her just that much closer, so he could kiss her more deeply, taste her more fully.

He eased his tongue between those inviting lips of hers and ran it, stroking, over the smooth, wet surfaces in there. Her tongue met his, shyly. He groaned at the feel of that.

She moaned low in her throat and he brought his other arm out from under the covers to pull her down onto the bed with him.

But she didn't allow that. Reluctantly, with a low sound of regret, she pulled away and straightened to her height. She gazed down at him, eyes so soft, mouth softer still. "I promised myself I wouldn't do that again."

He spoke low and roughly. "A promise like that just begs to be broken."

A low whine came from the doorway. He lifted his head to look. The bulldog and the white cat sat there, side by side.

Tessa chuckled. "They don't like it when I get out of bed in the middle of the night—go on," she told them. "I'll be up in a minute." They stood and stretched, more or less in unison, and then they turned and left the doorway—as if they'd understood exactly what she said. She touched his forehead on the uninjured side. "You're covered in sweat." She stroked his hair. "Are you uncomfortable?"

He saw a way to keep her with him longer—and went for it. When it came to her, he had no shame. "Yeah. You got an extra set of sheets, maybe?"

"It so happens I do. You want a shower, too?"

"A quick one. That would be great."

"How 'bout this? You go ahead and take that shower. While you're in there, I'll change the bed."

He could have offered to change the sheets himself, suggested that she leave them on the bed and he'd deal with it once he'd showered. But if he did that, she'd climb the stairs to join her dog and cat, leaving him alone, without her.

"Great," he said.

"Okay, then. You'll probably need to put fresh bandages on your knees. There's a first aid kit under the sink."

He thanked her. She left him to get the sheets and he threw back the covers and made for the shower, grabbing the sweats she'd loaned him from the rocker in the corner on the way. He went ahead and removed the bandages before getting in.

After he'd washed off the sweat and towel-dried, he checked the cuts on his knees again. They were no longer bleeding. The cuts were shallow, hardly more than bad scrapes. All the gauze and tape seemed like overkill. He used a couple of big adhesive pads instead. They worked fine.

When he returned to the bedroom, showered and wearing the sweats, she was spreading the blankets back on the bed. He helped her finish the job, then he sat in the rocker and put on the socks.

She shook her head. "I thought you were going back to bed."

He sent her a grin. "Soon. Right now, I'm in the mood to raid your refrigerator again—if that's all right with you."

"Of course it's all right. I've got some cold chicken, I think…."

He stood. "Now you're talkin'."

She led the way to the other room and started pulling stuff out of the fridge. She had cheese and she got some crackers from a cabinet. And there was the chicken. She put it all on the table. "Okay, then. Help yourself." She turned and started to go.

"You're leaving?" He tried to sound excessively needy and just marginally pitiful.

It worked. She faced him again. "You want me to stay?"

"Just for a few minutes, if you're not too tired…."

So she sat at the table with him while he wolfed down a chicken leg and thigh and a big hunk of cheese and several handfuls of Triscuits. He washed it all down with milk.

"Excellent," he said, setting his empty milk glass down with satisfied finality.

"Well, good." She reached for the plastic container of chicken and started to rise.

He caught her wrist—but gently, that time. "Leave it for a few minutes. Talk to me."

"Bill, really, it's late…."

He gestured toward the dark windows around them. "Come on. Live dangerously. You know you can sleep late— all day, if you want. Hear that wind?" It sighed and whistled around the eaves. And the snow was still coming down, piled over the sill out there, a few inches up the pane. "We're stuck in this house, at least for tomorrow. You can spend the day doing whatever you please."

Slowly, as if she doubted the wisdom of hanging around, she sat back in the chair. "Well, all right."

He asked, "What should we talk about?" though the question was purely rhetorical. He knew what he wanted to talk about: her. And her family. And that store she said she owned on Main Street. About her friends. About her hopes and her dreams.

But Tessa had other ideas. "What were you dreaming about?"

He frowned. "Dreaming?"

"This last time, when you woke up drenched in sweat and moaning, '*No*'?"

"Oh. That."

"Yes. That."

"I…" The headache, sleeping for a time, awoke in his head again. It began pounding faintly. He set himself the task of ignoring it. "Falling," he said. "I was falling."

"Falling, where?"

"I don't know. Out of the sky, I think—yeah. Out of the sky." He touched his temple, felt the wound there.

"Bill. Is your head hurting?"

If he told her it was, she'd insist he go back to bed. "No. Really. It's fine."

"You're sure?"

"Positive. There was…I think my family was there. For a while. Before the falling, I mean."

A smile lit her amazing face. Really, he could stare at her forever. She had the kind of face a man could look at every day for the rest of his life.

"Oh, Bill." Her voice held so much hope and wonder. "You remember your family?"

He shut his eyes, breathed in through his nose, let the air out slowly. The headache, which hadn't really gotten going this time, seemed to be receding. "It just seemed like…yeah. I think I was dreaming about my family. But now…"

"What?"

"It's gone. I can't remember."

She made a soft, sympathetic sound. "It's okay. It will come."

"Yeah," he said. "Right." And he was the one getting up then. He grabbed his empty plate and his glass and took them to the sink.

She rose, too, and started putting stuff away. He stuck the dishes in the dishwasher and then he straightened and stared out the window over the sink. Not that he could see out. What he saw was his own reflection, darkly, and wondered, *Who the hell are you?*

"Hey…" Her gentle voice in his ear, her soft hand on his shoulder.

He laid his hand over it. "It's okay. I'm okay…."

She asked, "Funny how we both keep telling each other everything's fine, huh?"

He turned and he was facing her and he couldn't stop himself. He reached for her. And the greatest thing happened. Instead of pushing him away, she wrapped her arms around him, good and tight. He buried his face in her neck and breathed in the perfect scent of her. He thought that maybe, if he never let her go, everything *would* be all right, somehow. If he held on forever, it wouldn't matter that he was a man without a name or any memory of his own life. *She* would be his life. She would be all he needed. From that night onward.

"I'm so damn scared," he whispered.

"I know." She squeezed him tighter. "I'm here. Right here with you."

He pressed his lips to her throat, once and then again. And then he was trailing a row of kisses, up over her chin to her mouth. She sighed as he kissed her and she didn't try to pull back.

He reveled in the moment. But he did know she had doubts. Yeah, he was shameless when it came to her. Not shameless enough, though, to lead her somewhere she wasn't sure she wanted to go.

In time, with dragging regret, he lifted his head. He took her by the shoulders. "We should get back to bed, huh?"

She studied his face, as if she couldn't stop seeking the answers she knew he didn't have. Finally, she nodded. "Yeah. Guess so." She felt for his hand. "Come on."

He followed where she took him, to her bedroom, where the sheets were clean and dry, the covers folded back, ready for him. All at once, he was so tired. Drained. Wrung out.

Gently, she guided him down to the mattress. He swung his feet up, without even the energy to get out of the purple sweats. She took off the socks, peeling them away, her warm fingers brushing his left ankle, her palm against his right sole.

She tossed the socks on the rocker in the corner. He saw the black boxers were there, too, hanging over the back. She must have brought them up from the basement when she went to get the sheets.

"Lie down," she told him. He obeyed and she tucked

the blankets around him. "There," she said tenderly, as if he were a child.

He knew he'd kept her awake long enough. Regretfully, he said the words that would release her. "Good night."

And that was when the lights went out.

Chapter Six

"Don't be afraid." Her voice, so close, out of the dark.

"It's okay," he said wryly. "I'm getting used to being in the dark. The lights might as well be out, too."

She chuckled. "Well, if we're lucky, in a minute or two, the power will come back on."

They waited. Without the clock, it was hard to tell how much time passed.

Finally, he heard her open a drawer in the nightstand. A moment later, a flashlight's beam cut the darkness. "I've got candles," she said. "And a few lanterns. And even a small generator in the basement that'll run the fridge and a couple of lights, if it comes to that."

"Sounds good."

"I'll just get you a lantern, then—so if you need light, you'll have it."

"A flashlight will do for the rest of the night, if you've got a spare."

"Sure. There's one in the kitchen. Be right back." She started to turn.

He had a brilliant idea. "Unless…"

"What?"

"Well. Why don't you just stay here for the rest of the night?"

She was frowning, her expression clearly visible even in the leftover spill from the flashlight's beam. "Here?"

He put up a hand like a witness swearing an oath. "I promise not to try and put the make on you—at least not until daylight."

Was she blushing? Maybe. "But I…" She paused to marshal her arguments.

He didn't give her the chance. "Think about it. Why go up and down the stairs in the dark to check on me when you can just stay here?"

She sank to the edge of the bed. "Well, I don't know. It just, um, seems like the best way…."

"Sleeping, Tessa. That's all we'll be doing." He held back the blanket enough that she could see he was fully dressed. "Me in these fine purple sweats and you in your snowman PJs. It's not a big deal, is it?"

She blew out a breath. "Not when you put it that way."

"So great. Come on." He patted the other side of the bed. "Stay here where you can keep an eye on me."

She made a low sound in her throat. "Yeah, well. You need keeping an eye on, that's for sure. In more ways than one."

He held her gaze for a moment. Then whispered, "Stay."

At last, with a shrug, she surrendered. He watched her,

the flashlight beam leading the way, as she circled the bed to the side nearest the window. "Hold this." She gave him the flashlight, dropped her slippers to the floor and climbed in, settling back on the pillow, her gold hair spilling across the white cotton pillowcase.

Tessa in bed with him.

Did it get any better than this?

She turned her head his way and wrinkled her nose at him. "All set. You can turn off the light now."

He really would have liked just to watch her lying there for a few minutes more. But she might get nervous if he did and start imagining he would try and jump her bones, in spite of his promise not to. So he switched off the light, put it in easy reach on the nightstand and stretched out beside her in the dark.

There was stillness between them. The sweet scent of her came to him, faintly. He shut his eyes. The mattress shifted slightly with the weight of her body. He drank in the soft, wakeful sound of her careful breathing.

Outside, the wind continued to sing under the eaves. He felt…peaceful. *At* peace in a way he hadn't been in the longest time.

He opened his eyes and stared into the darkness. The longest time? How long was that? He felt like a baby in so many ways. As if he'd been born only yesterday. At the same time he knew that, somewhere within him, the man he *had* been all the years of his life until now was waiting. He knew that his deeper, older self had rarely, if ever, been at peace in the way he was at this moment, in bed in the dark with the right woman beside him.

He knew he should let her sleep. But there was just too much he needed to know. "Tessa?"

"Hmm?"

"You should tell me a story—a bedtime story."

"Bedtime?" Her voice was throaty and sweet and threaded with humor. "It's way past your bedtime, Bill. It's got to be after four."

"So what? Live dangerously. Tell me a story."

"A story about what?"

"I don't know." But he did know. "Your family. Tell me a story about your family."

She sighed. "I wouldn't know where to begin. My family is…something else."

He waited. He could tell by the smile in her voice when she spoke that she had plenty of stories about her family. She only needed a minute or two to choose one.

Eventually, she did. "My Grandpa Oggie came to North Magdalene way back in the fifties and married my grandmother, Bathsheba Riley. They had four children— three wild, crazy, bad-acting Jones boys, one of whom is my dad. And one small, gorgeous, black-haired daughter, my Aunt Delilah."

He knew where she was headed. "And this is a story about Delilah Jones."

"It is. She's a schoolteacher, my aunt. And she was famous for miles around as a real man-hater. Nobody blamed her for hating men. My grandma, Bathsheba, died when Delilah was only eleven, leaving her with my troublesome grandpa, who ran the local bar."

"That would be The Hole in the Wall, right? I noticed it when I rode through town."

"The very one. And when Grandpa Oggie wasn't driving Aunt Delilah crazy with his smelly cigars and other totally annoying habits, there were her three bad-acting brothers to take up the slack. My dad and his brothers drank and fought and gambled their way through their teens and twenties. That house they all lived in growing up was a nightmare for Aunt Delilah, who was the only female around from such a young age and who spent way too much of her childhood trying to live a normal life, with her brothers coming in at all hours, drunk and swearing, half the time bleeding from some fight or other they'd been in—and expecting her to patch them up. It's really no surprise that she wanted nothing to do with a man once she finally got out on her own. She hardly dated. Folks in town all said there was no hope for her on the marriage front—mainly because she didn't *want* to get married. She had no plans to give up her pleasant single life. Why would she, when she'd only end up taking care of some man again?"

"Okay, so who *was* he when he came along?"

"Don't rush me, now. It's no fun if you rush it."

He laughed and dared to move his hand under the covers until he felt her flannel sleeve. He gave it a tug.

"Watch it," she warned.

"Couldn't resist."

"Oh, yeah, right. So anyway. By the time Aunt Delilah was in her thirties, Grandpa Oggie was starting to freak. He couldn't stand the idea of his only daughter being single and never giving him any grandkids. My grandpa, he's real big on love and marriage. And on grandkids— *having* them, I mean. Not taking care of them or anything. He's not a babysitting kind of grandpa."

"Tessa."

"Hmm?"

"Back to Sam and Delilah…"

"Right. Um, so, about then, while Grandpa's stewing over who he's gonna set Delilah up with, along comes Sam Fletcher, who's lived in town for fifteen or twenty years by then and owns his own store."

"Wait a minute."

"Yeah?"

"Sam. Delilah. Not their real names, right?"

"Real. True. Swear on my life. And he even cut off all his long hair for her, though eventually he grew it back again. But I'm getting ahead of myself—now, Sam, see, he was almost more like a Jones than a real Jones. He was friends with my dad and my uncles, he'd had a history of wildness, drinking and brawling and gambling and such. So around the time my Grandpa starts trying to decide who to set Delilah up with, Sam strolls into the bar and confides in my grandpa that he wants a wife."

"And your grandpa decides to get him and Delilah together."

"Oh, yeah. My grandpa, as usual, had no shame about it. He bribed, he begged, he coaxed, he threatened. And at first, Sam wasn't going for it. But somehow, once Sam started thinking about Aunt Delilah as a woman, he…couldn't stop. He really had his work cut out for him, though, because she'd never liked him and considered him just more of the same in the bad-acting man department…."

Over on his side of the bed, Bill let his eyes drift shut again as he listened to the story of how Sam Fletcher set out to win the man-hating schoolteacher, Delilah Jones. It was quite a tale and included all the gambling and brawling and drinking the men in Tessa's family were apparently famous for.

"And then," Tessa finished softly in a voice of wonder

and feminine satisfaction, "Sam scooped Delilah high in his arms and carried her out of The Hole the Wall with half the town watching, all whooping and hollering, thrilled at the glorious sight. They married soon after and they've been together ever since…" She lowered her voice to a whisper. "And I bet you're sound asleep by now."

He felt really smug. "Wrong. Great story."

"Why, thank you."

"But the part where he sweeps her off her feet and carries her out of the bar. That didn't really happen, did it?"

"It most certainly did," she said sharply.

He couldn't resist teasing, "You sure?"

She made a small, huffing sound. "I'll have you know that a lot of people were there and saw Sam carry her away. It happened just like I said."

"You love that part, don't you?"

A silence. Then, "So shoot me. I think it's romantic."

"Ah. Well, all right—and now Sam and Delilah have been married forever and they're still going strong."

"That's right."

"How many kids?"

"Well, that was the rocky part for them."

"No kids?"

"They wanted them. So bad. They tried and tried, but Aunt Delilah didn't get pregnant. Then, finally, about ten years ago, they adopted. And then she did get pregnant, after all. It was almost like, once they adopted their son and stopped trying so hard, nature took its course. So they have two. A boy and a girl. Ben and Daisy."

"That's good." He felt absurdly satisfied that Sam and Delilah's dream of a family had, in the end, come true.

She asked, "And can we please go to sleep now?"

"One last question."

"Oh, fine. What?"

"You, Tessa…"

"Yeah?"

"Are you maybe a little like your Aunt Delilah?"

"Me? Like my aunt? No way." And then she asked, cautiously, "How do you mean?"

"The tour bus driver, the one whose name you say you can't remember?"

She groaned. "Ugh. What's he got to do with anything?"

"Well, the way you described him, he didn't sound anything like the men in your family."

"He wasn't." Her voice was firm and sure. "Believe me."

"So, you're afraid of wild, manly men, too—just like Delilah was. Lucky for you, I'm not wild."

She muffled a sound and he knew she was stifling a laugh. "I notice you didn't say you're not manly."

"Here's a tip. Any man who tells you he's not manly? Run from him. Run away fast."

"Thanks," she said drily. "And no, I'm not afraid of wild, manly men. I'm just…not interested. But I haven't given up on men altogether."

"Whew."

"I'm serious, Bill."

"Oh, so am I."

"I…well, if you have to know, I go for the guy in the corner."

He wasn't following. "The corner of what?"

"You know, the guy who's sitting by himself, nursing a beer at the end of the bar. The quiet guy, who may not be all that good looking. The guy who's kind of shy with women."

He faked a snore.

"No, I don't find men like that boring, thank you very much." She made a sniffing sound. "I find them…sweet."

"Tessa."

"What?"

"You find them boring. And safe. And they pick up on that. But by then, you've built their confidence a little. So they go out and find someone who *really* likes them."

She groaned. "Now I have a question."

"Hit me with it."

"So you think maybe you're actually a shrink?"

He frowned at the dark ceiling. "Doubtful. Why?"

"Because that was…some analysis."

"Just an observation, that's all."

"I'll have you know I'm working hard right this minute to drum up a little outrage. I mean, do you hear what you're telling me? You're saying I don't even really like the guys I think I like. I should be *so* offended."

"But you're not."

"No." She sounded more than a little puzzled. "You're right. I'm…not."

He found her hand under the covers, wrapped his fingers around it and waited for her to pull away. But she didn't. He heard her sigh. Happier than he'd ever been in that life or the one he couldn't recall, he shut his eyes again and let sleep have him.

Someone was snoring.

He smiled to himself. So. She snored. Funny, but he found that charming. He found everything about her charming.

Carefully, he opened one eye. He was lying on his

back and there was gray daylight shining in the narrow gap between the curtains. Tessa lay beside him, asleep. So soft and beautiful. And not snoring, after all.

But somebody was.

Slowly, he turned his head the other way. And came face-to-face with the bulldog. Sound asleep. Snoring. Also drooling a little. How the hell the stumpy-legged animal had gotten up on the bed was a mystery to him.

Then he heard purring. He lifted his head off the pillow: the cat. She was curled up by his feet, awake, giving herself a bath. She paused in mid-lick, met his gaze, green eyes going low, the purr getting louder.

He let his head fall to the pillow again, realizing he didn't really care much if he had to sleep with a cat and a snoring, drooling bulldog. As long as he was sleeping with Tessa, too.

The clock by the bed was still dark, meaning the power remained out. Who knew what time it might be?

Not that it mattered a whole hell of a lot. He doubted they would get out of the house that day.

He frowned. Something was different....

It came to him: the headache that had been with him constantly, running the gamut between low-grade throb and drilling agony—was gone. He brought up a hand and touched the wound on his temple and tried to remember...who he really was, where he had come from.

Nothing. He still had mental access to exactly zip before the ride down the mountain in that semitruck. But there was good news: still no headache, not even when he tried to recall who he was.

He had no past.

But he also had no pain. At least not in his head. When he shifted a little, he winced at the aches all over his body from whatever rough punishment he had taken. Those aches would pass.

The headache had been the worst. And that was over, it seemed.

Happy in a deep and surprising way, given that he'd been born yesterday and had no clue how to find his way back to the man he'd once been, he turned onto his side, toward the window. And Tessa.

He watched her sleeping face until he drifted off again himself.

The next time he woke, there was whining.

And Tessa was sitting up beside him. She gave him the brightest, most amazing smile. "'Morning."

The whining came from the dog, which was off the bed and sitting on the floor, looking beyond pitiful.

He said, "I think your dog needs to go out."

"Yep." Tessa pushed back the covers and slid her feet into her slippers.

She stood. "Brr. I'll turn the heat up while I'm at it." She headed for the door. The dog, with a final, grateful moan, followed her out.

He got up, too, and used the bathroom, then opened the curtains at the bedroom window. The snow was still coming down. It was halfway up the windowpane. He heard the door to the basement shut and a minute later, Tessa appeared. Her cheeks were pink.

"Where's the dog?" he asked.

"I left her outside the basement door. My dad built me a breezeway down there, so she's more or less shielded from the snow. She can at least walk around a little and take care of business. I give her five minutes and she'll be yowling to get back in."

As if on cue, he heard barking down below.

Tessa grinned. "Be right back." She disappeared again.

He wandered out into the great room, where coals still glowed faintly in the woodstove. There was kindling in a small basket, logs in a sling. He realized he knew what to do to get the fire going.

Strange, having no past. He seemed to remember how to do things, how to walk and talk, how to feed and dress himself. How to read. How to build a fire. It was the man who had learned it all who was lost to him.

He was feeding the kindling in when Tessa and the bulldog reappeared. She went up to the sleeping loft first and came down with a travel clock. "Would you believe it's two-fifteen in the afternoon?" She showed him the dim face of the clock.

Still kneeling by the open stove door, he shrugged. "Feels like breakfast time to me."

"I'll get the coffee going." She went on into the kitchen.

He joined her once he had the logs in place on the kindling and the damper properly adjusted for greater air flow. She'd just set up what he recognized as a French press.

"Those make great coffee," he said, stepping up behind her to look over her shoulder, marveling again at the things he knew without knowing *how* he knew them.

She sent him a smile as she lit a burner. "Plus, they're perfect for when the power goes out." She set the glass pot on the fire. She still wore her snowman pajamas and her hair was tangled from sleep.

He breathed in the scent of her and accepted the fact that she was too tempting to resist—not that he *wanted* to resist her. He slid his arms around her.

When she didn't object to his embrace, he brushed her hair out of the way and kissed the pale skin of her neck. The fine, short, blond curls at her nape were downy soft, sweet-smelling as the rest of her.

With a sigh, she bent her head down for him. He guided her flannel collar aside so he could kiss the bumps at the top of her spine. It seemed so natural, so right, to ease his hands under her loose pajama top, to touch the skin of her waist, to feel the fine, sturdy shape of her ribcage.

And higher…

He cupped her full, firm breasts. So round and ripe. They fit his hands perfectly, but then, he'd known that they would. He brushed her already puckered nipples with his thumbs, felt them harden even more into tight, sweet buds and he smiled in pleasure at her body's response to his touch. She swayed against him with another long sigh. He buried his face in her soft gold hair.

But then, a tiny gasp escaped her. She shifted her weight away from him, caught his hands and gently guided them out from under the flannel shirt, slipping around to face him at the same time. She drew in an unsteady breath. Her cheeks were sweetly flushed. "I'll just…put some clothes on."

She escaped into the hallway before he could tell her he wished she wouldn't.

They had scrambled eggs and bacon, toast and the coffee, which was the best coffee he'd ever tasted. In this life or the one before. It *all* tasted so good. Really, everything—each breath he took, each glance across the table at the woman sitting there, each snowflake falling outside the windows—all of it was incredible, magical, completely amazing.

He told Tessa, "I can't get over all this."

"All what?" She sipped her coffee.

He spread his hands wide. "This. All of it. This snowy day in this house. With you."

She laughed. "I'm so pleased you're enjoying yourself."

"I am. Oh, yeah. More than words can say."

She set down her mug. "It does seem that you're feeling better."

"I do feel better. I feel great. Still a few aches and pains, but, well, I had this headache all day yesterday. Not anymore. It's gone."

"Terrific. Any…memories yet?"

"Not a damn one." He said it cheerfully.

She sipped more coffee. "Well, you've certainly got the right attitude about it."

He slumped back in his chair, his buoyant mood suddenly less so. "What? You think I should be more freaked out, right?"

That time she set the mug down a little harder. "Absolutely not. I'm glad you feel better. I'm just…" She shut her eyes, breathed in through her nose. When she looked at him again, her eyes were troubled, but she put on a smile. "Listen. You're right. It doesn't hurt to look on the bright side. It's good. Truly. So much wiser than worrying."

He understood then. "Tessa."

She bit her lip, glanced toward the window where the snow kept piling up. The gray light from outside couldn't dim the warm color of her smooth, tempting skin. She had lips made for kissing, upturned at the corners, full and inviting.

When she'd left him to change, she'd put on jeans and a green sweater. Her hair, brushed smooth, fell loose on her shoulders, gold against the green.

He thought about touching her, about taking off the sweater and those snug faded jeans, about kissing those breasts of hers that felt so good in his hands, about making love to her, naked, in the gray light of the storm.

Softly, she confessed, "I only, well, I worry that if something goes wrong—"

"It won't." He spoke in a voice that held no room for doubt. What, after all, was the point of doubting? They weren't going anywhere until the snow let up, so why worry about something they couldn't control? "I'm going to be okay. You've got the perfect house to be stuck in during a blizzard. We're comfortable, even without electricity. And then there's you...."

Her brows had drawn together. "Me."

"You." He rose. "You're the best thing about this whole situation."

She watched him come to her, eyes so wide, green as new grass. He stood above her and touched her soft cheek, lifted her chin with a finger.

"I...I like you, too," she said, her voice heavy with equal parts desire and regret. "Maybe too much."

"Uh-uh," he told her. "Between you and me, there is no such thing as too much." He touched her shoulder. "Come up here to me where I can kiss you. Come on."

"Oh see, this is the thing. I don't think we should be, you know, getting too crazy or anything...."

"This is not crazy. This is completely sane. The sanest thing either of us has ever done."

"It's the strangest thing."

"What is?"

"When you talk like that, I believe you."

"Good."

"Am I a fool, Bill?"

"No way. You're the least foolish person I've ever known, in this life or the one I can't remember. Come on."

Slowly, she stood. When she reached her full height, he took her waist between his hands. Touching her was everything. And holding her with both hands had the added benefit of keeping her from edging away.

With charming reluctance, she admitted, "I…feel so close to you. It's beyond strange. Like I've known you forever. As if every other man I've gone out with was just a…shadow. A placeholder. While I was waiting for you."

"That's it exactly," he whispered.

"But I've never been all that smart about men, you know?"

"Everything's different now. Now, you're with me."

"Oh, I do want to believe that."

"So do it. Believe it."

"I have to keep reminding myself that we only just met."

Slowly, he shook his head. "No, you don't."

"Yeah. I do. If I don't, well, anything might happen."

"And isn't that great?"

"Bill, I…" Her voice trailed off. She whispered, "Don't."

"Don't what?"

"Don't…look at me like that. Don't touch me like that."

He frowned. What she said seemed impossible. "You're serious? You want me to stop?"

"We *should* stop. You're in no condition to—"

He silenced her with a gentle finger against her mouth. "Uh-uh. Listen."

She swallowed, flustered in the sweetest way. "I…what?"

"If you don't want to make love with me, fine. I get that. I may not like it, but it makes sense. No matter that you say you feel like you've known me forever, you haven't. The reality is what you said a minute ago. You met me yesterday. And I was not at my best. So if you need time to be sure, take it. If you decide in the end you're just not going there, I'll hate it. But I can live with it. It's your right. I'm good with that." He dared a slow smile. "Not that I'll stop trying to convince you otherwise."

"I—"

"Shh." He pressed his finger to her lips again. "Not finished."

A breathless sound. "Sorry…"

"My point is, if you want to say no, say it for yourself. Let me decide for myself what I'm ready for."

"But yesterday you were unconscious for hours. You've been seriously injured. You still don't even know who you are."

"I know what I want. I know what I feel. And right now, this moment? *This* is what counts, Tessa. This is what matters."

Her thick, gold lashes swept down and then slowly up again. She met his gaze. "All right. I see your point. Of course you're the one who knows how much better you feel, what you're…well enough to be doing."

He rubbed her strong, slightly pointed chin with his thumb. "Well, okay then. So the question remains. Do you want me to stop?"

"I…" Her eyes shone with eagerness, telling him exactly what he wanted to hear, in spite of the fact that she hadn't said it yet. And then she confirmed what he already knew. She straightened those broad shoulders and tipped her chin high. "No. Never. Never stop."

Chapter Seven

Relief flowed through him, followed by a hot rush of desire. His knees felt weak.

They didn't have to stop. She didn't *want* him to stop.

He *had* to kiss her. And he did. But with care, with…gentleness. He brushed her lips with his, holding himself back, though his body urged him on. He knew he'd been pushing her too fast, so he made a serious effort to show her he could take things slow.

But then, with a small, soft cry, she opened for him, offering him the deepest kind of kiss. And he was lost. He yanked her close with a groan. Reveling in the warm, soft feel of her body against him, he slid his tongue beyond her parted lips and found it wet and sweet in there, flavored with coffee. And so hot.

She let out a low cry and surged up to wrap her arms around his neck.

That did it. So much for taking it slow. Already, he was fully aroused, aching, *hurting* with need for her.

He kissed her and went on kissing her, deeply and thoroughly, holding her tight in his hungry embrace, sweeping a hand down to cup her round bottom. She gasped when he did that.

But she didn't push him away. His senses on fire, his body needing hers as urgently as he needed to draw his next breath, he pressed her even more firmly into him, pushing his hips against her at the same time, so she could feel how much he wanted her.

Her breathing changed, grew shallow and quick, as he went on kissing her, running his hands up and down the sleek, strong shape of her back, caressing the twin inward curves at her waist that flared outward so temptingly to her hips. She was lifting up and into him now, pushing her sex against him, wordlessly offering him exactly what he needed, what he was starving for.

Had he really lived without the taste of her all his life until yesterday? Had he lived without the strength and softness of her filling his arms, the scent of her that was so right, so perfectly suited to him?

It must have been one damn miserable life, the one he'd led up until now. A life without her in it. Who wanted that?

He didn't.

He caught her face between his hands and kissed her even more deeply, penetrating and retreating, mimicking the pulse of lovemaking. She moaned into his mouth. He shut his eyes and drank from her.

It wasn't enough. He wanted her, *all* of her. He put his hands to her waist again, began waltzing her backward, toward the sofa in the great room.

She went where he guided her, those strong, long-fingered hands of hers all over him, caressing his shoulders, his chest, sliding lower to encircle his waist.

And then even lower…

She touched him, cupping him fully over the sweatpants she'd given him to wear. He groaned into her mouth as she brushed her warm palm along the hard, hungry length of him. She made him crazy. She made him burn.

He'd forgotten his goal of getting her prone on the couch. He couldn't think when she touched him that way. He stopped dancing her backward and they stood, mouths locked in an endless kiss, in the middle of the floor in front of the stove he'd so carefully stoked a while before. He groaned again as she slid her hand up, under the waist of the sweatshirt. She pressed her palm to his belly, as if steadying him for what was to come.

If she didn't wrap her fingers around him soon, he would go crazy. He caught her wrist, flattened his hand over hers, moaned his need deep in his throat.

She knew. She understood. She went on kissing him, driving him wild with that soft mouth of hers, while she eased her fingers under the elastic at his waist.

It was almost enough, the warm pads of her fingers against his lower belly, stroking, rubbing where he knew that dark bruise was. He felt the tenderness of the flesh there. But only in passing. Mostly, he felt hunger. He was on fire for her.

A second later, her fingers slid into the thick nest of hair at the apex of his thighs…and lower still.

And then it happened. She found him, took him, curling her hand firmly around the length of him.

He thought for sure he would die then. Die of pure pleasure, moaning her name.

The pleasure she gave him intensified. She stroked him, learning the shape and the feel of him, her fingers working the shaft and then sliding up and over the head. He felt her thumb trace the slit there, drawing up thick, creamy moisture that she spread over him, using her palm, then wrapping her fingers tight on the length again, but now with the wetness to make each caress a hot glide.

It was heaven. A pleasure so pure and fine. Too bad if he let her keep on, he would lose it, then and there. And that wouldn't be right.

Not for their first time. Uh-uh. Their first time had to be special. It couldn't be rushed.

With sharp regret, he reached down and stilled her hand. "Too...fast. Not yet." He breathed the words against her parted lips.

With a sigh, she released him.

He took her face in his hands. "I should ask..."

She searched his eyes. "What?" Her lips were redder, swollen with the kisses they'd shared. He wanted only to claim them again.

But the question he'd yet to ask did matter. He said softly, "Condoms?"

She drew in a shaky breath and nodded. "In the bedroom. Back of a drawer in the nightstand."

"Good." He took her hand and headed for the other room. Fast. "Where?" he asked when they stood by the bed.

She pulled open the second drawer, reached into the back and brought out a whole box of them. Unopened. "Here you go. I've got plenty." She turned his hand over and put the box in his waiting palm.

He dropped to the side of the bed and checked the expiration date: still good. And then he grinned up at her. "So you've been expecting me, huh?"

She moved in close. He spread his thighs to accommodate her. Gently, she combed the hair at his temple with her fingers, holding his gaze, her mouth soft and ripe as forbidden fruit. "Oh, yes. I was expecting you, all right. Maybe I didn't know it, but I've been expecting you…forever."

He turned his face into her palm and kissed the very center of it. "Tessa, I'm here." He reached over, set the box on the nightstand, and then took her hips between his hands. "Right here."

"I'm so glad." She bent and gave him her mouth. Straining toward her, he kissed her.

He could never get enough of her kisses, of her sweet, yearning sighs. The kiss went on, endless and amazing as all the other kisses she'd given him.

As they kissed, they undressed each other. He unzipped her jeans and shimmied them down. She kicked her flat shoes behind her, pushed her panties down, too. They laughed together, still kissing, as she wiggled the jeans and panties off the rest of the way.

They had to break the kiss to get her sweater off. He took advantage of the moment to get rid of the sweats, top and bottom, and to pull off the fat socks she'd given him and toss them away.

At last, he was naked. She had only her bra. It was yellow as spring sunshine. He sat back down on the edge of the bed and reached up to cup her breasts. "Perfect," he whispered. She slid a hand behind her and undid the clasp.

The bra fell loose under his palms. He slipped his

thumbs in, touched her hard, hot nipples. She let her head fall back on a moan.

Admiring the shape of her—the singing curve of her neck, the strong silhouette of her shoulders—he traced the lacy cups upward, to the straps, which he guided, one finger on each, down the sleek, softly muscled length of her arms. She let it drop away.

And finally, she was naked. And he was naked.

In the pearly light that shone in the window, he admired her, so tall and strong, and yet soft, too, with rounded belly and full breasts. He'd never seen anything so right. So beautiful. As Tessa, tall and curvy and proud, standing there, before him.

He whispered it to her. "Beautiful. You are so beautiful."

She caressed his shoulder. "No. *You.* You're beautiful."

He didn't argue. What did it matter? He knew what he saw when he looked at her. And if she thought he was beautiful, too, well, that meant they both had something really good to look at.

He touched her left breast, lightly, tracing the fine, rounded curve, loving the delicate tracery of veins below the surface. He cupped it as he had before, leaning close. She reached for him then and gathered him against her, so he could taste her, take that hard, tempting nipple into his mouth.

He sucked, running his tongue in a circle around the aureole, then sucking some more, drawing deep. She pulled him closer against her and moaned her pleasure at the wet caress of his tongue on her flesh.

Slowly, he thought. *Go slow. Give it time...*

Life was so fragile. He, of all men, knew that too well. Right then, in her bedroom, his head against her bare breasts, he had everything. All that mattered, right here. With her. He had her warm body and her tender sighs, her kisses, her hungry cries of need and pleasure.

It was so good. It couldn't have been more right.

He took her gently by the shoulders and she straightened to her height. Her eyes, looking down into his, were moss-green and shining. She smiled at him.

And he traced a line down the center of her, between her full, deep breasts, over the rounded curve of her belly, to the sweet space between her thighs and the dark-gold curls there. He petted those curls, easing his fingers into them, loving the shine of them, the warmth, the promise.

Lower.

He went lower. She gasped as he parted her. And she swayed a little on her feet.

"Brace your hands on my shoulders."

She did, with a low moan.

"Open. Open for me…"

She eased her legs apart until they brushed his spread thighs.

"Perfect," he whispered.

She answered by gripping his shoulders harder and letting her head fall back with a whimper that turned into a moan.

Wet. She was so wet for him. He found the center of her arousal and he played it with his thumb, while with his fingers, he touched her, exploring the slippery, secret folds, learning her pleasure—what she wanted. What she craved.

She responded, eager and open in lovemaking, as he'd somehow known she would be, moving her hips in time with his stroking hand, tossing that gold hair, moaning the name he'd told her to call him.

Her breath caught. She went still, the muscles in her strong thighs drawing tight, her fingers clutching his shoulders. He took her body's signal, stroking deeply—and then holding.

There. Yes. He smiled as he felt the pulsing start. He cupped her, tightly, feeling the tender explosion of her climax, whispering the two words that filled his mind, "Yes. Tessa. Yes…"

With a shuddering sigh, she sagged toward him. He reached up to gather her close, to stroke her back, bury his face in her hair.

She was panting. And then she giggled.

"What?" He pressed a kiss to the side of her neck.

"Don't…believe," she whispered. "…amazing."

"Good. Amazing is good."

"Amazing is excellent," she declared, catching her breath. "And I really need to lie down now."

He smoothed her wild hair aside and spoke in her ear. "Not yet."

She groaned. "What now?"

He took her hips and gently pushed her backward. "This…" He knelt on the bedside rug before her. "This…" And he kissed her, kissed those musky gold-brown curls.

She stood so still, her whole body quivering. And then, as she gave herself up to him, she threaded her hands into his hair. "Oh!" The word came out on a cry that faded down to a silvery whisper of joy. "Oh, my goodness…" She braced her legs a fraction wider.

Again, she used his shoulders for support.

And he kissed her. Deeply. The musky, slick-wet taste of her was in his mouth. The heavy, arousing scent of her sex was on him. And in him. He couldn't get enough of her.

Never. Never enough.

She went over the moon again, whimpering, sighing. He held up his arms to her as she rocked on her feet and then crumpled toward him.

Rising, he caught her. He swept her up as if she weighed nothing. Turning, in two steps, he was at the bed.

He laid her down, carefully, sharply aware that nothing in the world mattered as much as this woman who had saved him. This woman who looked at him through wide-open eyes, who knew she should be wary of him—but wasn't, couldn't be. This woman who laughed and lived and loved full-out, no holding back.

He laid her down and blessed the forces that had brought him to her door, blessed the unknown, life-threatening event that had taken who he really was from him. He knew then, with a certainty he couldn't explain, that the man he'd been before would never in a thousand years have found her. The man he'd been before would have walked right past her on the street, unknowing, unseeing, arrogant and unaware that his only hope had been so near he could have reached out and touched her.

Naked on the white sheet, she gave him a smile. Her eyes shone, almost more gold than green at that moment. "You look…so sad."

He sat on the bed beside her, stroked her silky hair, smoothing it on the white pillow. "Not sad. Never sad."

She touched one of the bruises on his chest, then tracked the trail of hair there downward to the band of bruising low on his abdomen. "Hurts?"

He shook his head. "I've never felt better, never felt more alive."

She touched his forehead, near the injury that had taken his memory. "Then why the sad look?"

He lifted a shoulder in a half shrug. "Life, I guess. It's damn scary, the things that happen. The things you can miss if you're not paying attention."

Her soft hand slid around to clasp his neck. "Oh, yes. You're right. It's so important. To pay attention."

He bent close, breathed in her scent, kissed the slope of her breast. "*This* is what matters…."

"Oh, yes."

"You. Me. Now."

"Yes…" She scooted over to the far pillow, and patted the space where she had been.

Swinging his legs up, he stretched out beside her. She turned to him, laid a hand on his chest, palm flat. Her face wore a look of concentration. He knew she was feeling the beat of his heart.

Then, with a sigh, she scooted closer and laid her head where her hand had been. "Heaven," she said on a breath.

"Paradise," he answered, stroking her hair.

She lifted her head and scooted up so they were face-to-face, her hair falling around them, surrounding them in a veil of gold. Her mouth touched his. Yes. Paradise. They kissed, long and deep.

In time, she reached over him for the box on the nightstand. She rose up and sat cross-legged and peeled back the top flap. He saw two rows of neat pouches waiting inside.

"Hmm," she said, pressing a finger to her chin. "Which one should I choose?"

He admired the twin globes of her breasts, the roundness of her belly, the strength in her thighs, the hint of wet pink showing boldly beneath the thatch of dark-blond curls. Just looking at her, he was hard. And getting harder. "Pick one. Quick. Before I explode."

"Well, now." She ran her finger along the two rows, chose one, held it up. "Hmm." She eyed his erection, then frowned at the condom again. "I'm just not sure it will fit."

A burst of laughter escaped him. And in spite of his growing need to bury himself inside her, he raised his arms and laced his hands behind his head. "What is it about you?"

She was still frowning at the condom, but she spared him a glance and asked, all innocence, "Me?"

"Somehow, you always know the right thing to say to a man."

"My stepmother's a lady," she said, as if that explained everything. "Gina brought me up right."

"Good to know—and Tessa."

"Hmm?"

"That one will do fine." He held out his hand. "Give it here."

She clutched it to those beautiful breasts of hers. "No. Really. Allow me."

He gritted his teeth, but he surrendered. "Have it your way."

"I intend to."

"Make it quick."

"Well, all right." She lifted up on her knees and stretched across him to set the box back on the nightstand. Her breasts swung free, begging for his touch. He reached for one.

She caught his hand, kissed the back of it, gently pushed it away. "Patience."

He grunted. "Losing that. Fast."

She sat back on the bed again and ripped open the condom pouch with her white, strong teeth. She peeled back the wrapper.

He lifted his head off the pillow and glared at her. "You're killing me, you know that?"

"Oh, well, yes." She glanced up, smiling sweetly. "That's the plan. But in a good way, I promise. A very, very good way."

He groaned and let his head fall back, shutting his eyes, determined to wait her out at the same time as he doubted that he could.

She said, "Wait right there. Keep your eyes closed."

He swore, darkly, in reply. But he did wait, with his eyes shut as she'd commanded. He felt the bed shift, heard the soft sound of her feet padding across the floor. A drawer slid open and then shut.

The mattress shifted again with her return. She touched his cheek with a soft, light cloth.

"What?" He opened his eyes and saw she held a red scarf.

"Blindfold?" She dangled it above his head. "What do you think?"

He could see the possibilities and they were good ones. "Me? Or you?"

She lowered the silky fabric to his chest and dragged it down the center of him. "You." She circled his erection with it.

He asked, raggedly, "Uh. What brought this on?"

"I don't know. It was just a thought. But maybe you don't—"

He caught her wrist. "Do it."

"You sure?"

"I'm sure of only one thing. I want you. Bad. Now. And however you want me, it's okay. Do it."

"Well, then." She rolled the scarf and put it over his eyes. "Lift up." He obeyed and she tied it behind his head, moving the knot to the side, out of his way. "Excellent," she said, when she gently guided his head back down on the pillow.

He felt vaguely foolish: naked. Blindfolded. And yet somehow, even more aroused than before. "What did you do with the condom?"

"Thus, the blindfold," her voice teased in his ear. "You manly men always want to run the show. You need to give a girl a chance."

"Uh, fine. Take charge. I'm all yours."

"That's the spirit."

"But…you didn't answer my question."

"I have it," she whispered. "And I'll use it. I promise. That's all you need to know." She bit his earlobe, lightly.

"Yes, ma'am," he answered on a groan, faking obedience for all he was worth.

He felt her hand, lightly, caressing his chest, sending shivers of need through him. He willed those warm, gentle fingers of hers to move downward.

They did. She wrapped her hand around him. Tight. He groaned, lifting his hips for more.

She took him in her mouth, drawing him, by agonizing degrees into the wet, slick cave beyond her lips, working her tongue around him. Sucking, teasing him with the careful scrape of her teeth.

His body bowed up off the mattress. She guided him down and she went on with that mouth of hers, driving him to the brink, but not quite letting him go over. She took him to the edge, once and then again and yet again. Pushing him further than he ever dreamed he could go, somehow instinctively knowing when to hold back to keep him from reaching the finish.

He was wild for her by then, tossing his head on the pillow, arms spread, gripping handfuls of sheet, willing himself not to reach for her, not to flip her hard to her back and roll her beneath him.

In the end, she pulled her mouth away. He groaned at the loss of that sweet, hot, sucking wetness.

But then he felt the bed move as she rose up. A silky thigh touched him on either side and he knew that she straddled him, up on her knees. He could feel her looking down at him. He wanted to see that so bad, her body above him, her eyes shining, a soft smile on her lips.

But he didn't lift the blindfold. He let her lead the way as he'd promised he would. He didn't steal her mastery from her.

"Tessa," he whispered, blind. Yearning. "Tessa. Please…"

"Yes," she told him. "Oh, yes. I promise you. Yes. Now…" And he felt her tender touch on him, felt her slide the protection over him, rolling it smoothly, from the crown and lower, all the way to the base.

He held a groan of pleasured agony tight inside his chest as she encircled him with her fingers again, steadying him into position. And then, at last, she came down onto him, her body opening fully to him, taking him into herself, smooth and deep and slow.

"Oh…" She moaned when he filled her fully. "Oh, yes. Exactly…" Her clever internal muscles tightened, and he couldn't hold back. He loosed that groan he'd held tight in his chest. "You feel so good," she told him, bracing her palms on his shoulders, her head bent close so her hair trailed across his chest and her breath warmed his skin. "Never in my life, like this," she whispered.

He understood. "The best. So good…" The pleasure was too much. It became impossible for him to remain completely passive. He grabbed her hips between his hands and pushed up harder into all that sweetness, into the heaven that was her body.

She moaned, taking him deeper still. Oh, he wanted to see that—the sight of them, joined.

But he left the blindfold in place. He let his other senses carry him: scent, sensation, sound. Touch. And the taste of her kisses. They were enough. For now.

Her body was liquid, moving over his, like an ocean. Like a universe in which he was only one blazing, burning star. He dared to caress her, his hand moving upward over the sleek shape of her back. When she allowed that, he cupped her breasts. The hard nipples teased his palms.

"More," he whispered. "All of you."

"Yes," she answered. "Oh, yes. Everything. Nothing held back." She moaned as he caught her nipples, tugging.

And he let his touch wander, down over her ribs, and inward. He touched her most sensitive spot, rubbing, pleasuring her, as she rode him. She cried out at that.

He surged up into her, wanting more of her. All of her, all around him. She was life and goodness, breath. And hope. Everything he hadn't understood that he needed, in that past life that was lost to him, the life where, he knew, he'd been a different man than now.

He felt her rising to her climax. And he was rising too, going liquid. Molten.

Supernova.

His whole body trembled. And he couldn't stop himself. He had to see her, finally, at the end.

He reached up and ripped off the blindfold. And there she was, above him, the sight of her thrilling him, as glorious and free as he had known her to be. Her head thrown back, her body straining, shining with sweat, she hit the finish with a guttural cry. She moaned the name he'd called himself.

He heard himself correct her. "Asher. My name is Ash…"

She lowered her head and her eyes opened, dazed with fulfillment, but wondering, too. "Ash?"

And then he was following her over the edge. He grabbed her hips and held her down hard on him as the universe turned inside-out and his body pulsed, electric.

He knew everything, for that blinding moment. He knew it all. Saw it all: who he had been, the folly of his old life, the cataclysm that had brought him here, to this one special woman's tender, loving arms.

He shut his eyes as ecstasy claimed him. The pulse of his finish took him over, filling the world. Emptying him out.

Leaving him limp, fully satisfied.

And unknowing, once more.

Chapter Eight

"Asher?" she asked a little later, when they lay together, naked, in the fading light of late afternoon.

He turned his head lazily her way. "What?"

"You said your name was Asher. Ash, you said. 'My name is Ash.'"

"I did?"

Now she was frowning, her smooth brows drawn together. "You don't remember?"

He shut his eyes, tried to recall. "There was…something, I guess. A flash, no more."

"And?" Her hopeful tone hurt almost as much as the big, dark empty place where his memory should have been. He knew she wanted the best for him, wanted him whole. And he only wanted to give her all she desired.

But this, who he really was? If he'd known, for a moment, he knew no more. "Sorry," he said. "It's gone."

"Ash…" She tried the name again, as if learning its taste on her tongue. "I like it. It's a little sad. A little…lonely. And so very sexy. Just like you."

"Lonely and sad, huh? Gee, thanks."

"And sexy," she reminded him. "Don't forget that."

He rose up on an elbow so he could look down into her green eyes. "You're so beautiful." He caught a curl of her hair and rubbed it between his thumb and forefinger. "So warm. So alive…"

"Ash," she said again, wearing that tender, hopeful look. "Shall I call you that, then?"

He dropped to his back again and stared at the ceiling. "No."

"But if it's your—"

"Bill," he cut in flatly. "Just Bill. For now."

Then she was the one levering up, bending over him. "Are you angry?"

"Angry?" He studied her face. He could never get enough of looking at her. "At you? Never."

"Good." She touched his chin, trailed a finger down over his throat to his chest. She laid her palm flat, over his heart. "Good," she repeated, with a soft sigh.

He touched her hair, stroking, then guided her head down to rest on his chest. She relaxed against him. He knew he'd been curt. He tried again. "It's only that, until I know for sure what my name was before, I'd rather just go with one I chose for myself." It was more than that, though he didn't know how to tell her. It was…his powerlessness in the face of the blankness within. The glimmers of light, of sensing the man he'd been before, of memory…they either faded to darkness or left him with yet more questions to which he had no answers.

She lifted her head to meet his eyes. "Okay. Bill." They shared a smile. And then she shrugged. "But it *is* something, you know? You did remember *something* there, for a minute or two. That's good. And you remembered in your dreams, too. Right?"

"Seems like it."

"So maybe your memory is trying to come back."

"Too bad it's not succeeding all that well."

"Give it time."

He traced the line of her hair where it curved along her cheek. "Like I've got a choice."

"It'll come back to you. I know it will."

He slipped his hand around the back of her neck and pulled her sweet lips down so they brushed his. "Let's talk about something else."

She lay halfway across his body and must have felt him hardening. She grinned. A very naughty grin. "I'll bet I know what."

He took her mouth then, hard, plunging his tongue in, rolling as he did it, so she was beneath him. She felt really good there. He lifted his lips from hers, but only far enough to tell her, "My turn to be on top."

She stroked his hip and shifted temptingly under his weight. "Do you hear me arguing?"

"Kiss me."

She offered her mouth to him. He took it, slowly, this time, with care. With tenderness.

In no time, he was reaching for the box on the night-stand again.

Tessa could have lain in bed beside him forever. But after they made love that second time, she couldn't help but notice that the light outside was starting to fade.

And Mona Lou and Gigi were sitting in the doorway again, looking hopeful that soon they'd be getting fed.

He lay on his stomach, his head on his powerful arms. She kissed his shoulder, murmured against his warm flesh, "Don't panic. Make no sudden moves. But there are starving animals nearby."

"Uh-oh."

She stole a moment to admire him. Dear Lord, he was perfect. She'd never seen a butt like that up close and personal before.

He lifted his head and peered at her sideways. "What are you looking at?"

"Do you know you have a truly amazing butt?"

He buried his head in his arms again. "Glad you like it."

She slapped him lightly on all that amazingness. "We have to get up."

"Why?" He rolled over then. Yet more amazingness to admire.

"Mona and Gigi want dinner. And there's the no-electricity problem. We need to get out the lanterns and candles for when it gets dark—which will be soon. And to get the generator going so the fridge won't defrost."

"Ugh," he said. "Just when I was thinking of making love to you again."

She bent and kissed him, a quick one. "Hold that thought."

He caught her arm. "I will. Believe me."

She looked in those eyes that were the most astonishingly beautiful cobalt blue and she *did* believe him. He wanted her as much as she wanted him. And that was a whole lot.

Ash, she thought. She knew that had to be his name.

From now on, silently, she would call him that. Asher. Ash. Oh, yes.

But if he wanted to be called Bill to his face, fine. It must be terrible for him, not knowing who he really was. She was all for anything that made it easier on him. Including calling him by the name he'd given himself.

"Bill," she said. "Come on. Let's get up. We've got work to do."

So they fell out of bed and pulled on their clothes. He fed the dog and cat as she got out the lanterns and the candles and put them on the table, ready to go.

His arms came around her from behind and he kissed the side of her neck. "The animals are fed. Now what?"

She turned in his embrace and rested her hands on his shoulders. "We hook up the generator."

"You make it sound ominous."

"It's just a pain, that's all." She moved in closer, linking her arms around his neck. "Kiss me first?"

"No need to ask." He lowered his mouth and she lifted hers. Their lips met—and at that exact moment, the lights came on.

They pulled back at the same time, laughing as the refrigerator started up, a low, mechanical hum.

"Would you look at that?" he said. "All it took was a kiss."

She beamed at him. "I should check the phone, too. You never know." She hurried over there and grabbed it off the wall, hope rising. But when she put it to her ear, there was nothing but silence. She shook her head.

"No go, huh?"

"Not yet." She hung up.

"Don't worry." He looked at her so hopefully. "We're safe and warm. And I'm doing fine. I may not know who

I am yet, but I do feel a whole hell of a lot better than I did twenty-four hours ago."

He did seem better, she thought. Much better, really. Could a man about to fall into a deadly coma from a subdural hematoma make passionate, thrilling love all afternoon? It hardly seemed likely. But then again, she was no expert on such things.

"What?" he asked. "I don't seem better to you?"

She realized she'd been silent too long. He needed a reassuring reply. "You do."

"Then why do you look worried?"

"I'm not." It was a lie, but a small one. She was still concerned—just not as much as before. "And the snow could stop any time now. We'll be out of here and getting you to a doctor before you know it."

"Right," he said, but his gaze slid away.

"It would be nice, in a way," she said softly, "to stay here forever, just the two of us…."

He still didn't meet her eyes. He seemed to be watching the snow falling beyond the window by the table. "Yeah."

"It's turned out to be…kind of magical, you know?"

He made a low noise of agreement. And continued to stare at the storm outside.

She sighed. "Bill. Are you okay? Did I say something…to upset you?"

And that did it. He turned his head to her at last and stared at her through haunted eyes. "A lot about my situation bothers me. But not you. You just…make me happy. You give me hope."

She went to him with a cry and he gathered her close. He whispered, "It's strange…."

"What?" She hugged him tight. "Tell me."

He stroked her hair. "I'm happy, here, with you. And that seems…strange to me."

She lifted her head from the crook of his shoulder so that she could see his face. "Being happy seems strange?"

"Yeah. It does. I don't think I was happy…before. Maybe I had been happy, when I was a kid. But later, as a grown man, I think I'd made some bad choices, you know?" At her nod, he went on. "And that man, whoever I was before, I resent him a little. I don't want to be him again. I don't want to lose this, to lose *us*."

"You won't," she promised, knowing as she said those words that it was a vow she had no right to make. When his old self, the one named Ash, awakened, everything could change. They could so easily end up apart, with him returning to his old life, and Tessa going on as before.

Then again, what if his memory never returned?

She shut her eyes tight. There were too many questions and no real answers. Better to focus on what was, on the two of them, together, right now. She had chosen to be with him, and she would. Fully. For as long as this magical time lasted.

"Just hold me," she whispered.

And he did, so tenderly, for the longest time.

Eventually, they put the lanterns and candles away and then took Mona downstairs for a short trip outside. When they came back up, Tessa prepared a simple meal. They ate.

And then they watched the news in the great room, sitting on the sofa with their arms wrapped around each other, Mona on one side, Gigi on the other. The weather report said the storm would continue on into tomorrow, with chances of clearing possible by the afternoon.

Again, there was no news of a man going missing in the mountains.

He pushed the mute button when the commercial came on. "See? Nothing. No missing persons fitting my description—no missing persons at all. Maybe I'm imagining the man I once was. Maybe I don't exist. Maybe I never did."

She lifted her head from his shoulder. His eyes were hooded, hard to read. She ached for him. But she made herself speak firmly. "Take my word. You exist."

He grunted. "You sound so sure."

"There are any number of explanations for why no one has reported you missing yet."

"Like?"

"Maybe they…don't know you're gone. Or maybe you went missing from somewhere else—you know, you were kidnapped, maybe. And they took you up into the mountains."

"They?" He lifted an eyebrow.

"It's just a thought, just a…possibility."

"And then I escaped, right? I was in such a hurry to get away, I left my memory behind."

"I'm serious. Truly."

"You may not believe it, but so am I."

She cast about for a way—any way—to reassure him. "When we get out of here, once you've been to the clinic, we'll talk to my Uncle Jack. He's the county sheriff. He'll have the resources to find out more. He can get your description out on an All Points Bulletin, or whatever they call it."

"Great. I guess."

She searched his face and didn't know what to say. "You're scared," she told him softly. "It's natural."

"I'm…a blank. A damn blank. And yeah. It scares me." He pulled away from her and stood. "Fine. As soon as we get out of here, I'll go to the clinic. I'll talk to your Uncle Jack. Anything else?"

She stared up at him, seeking the right words, knowing there was nothing she could say to make it all better. "You're angry with me. I'm so sorry. I'm just trying to figure out what we can do, to make sure you're okay. To find out who you really are."

He glared at her for a moment. And then the heat and anger seemed to drain away. His broad shoulders slumped. "Don't be sorry. *I'm* sorry." His voice was low, ragged with pain. He tossed the remote on the coffee table and left her.

She watched him walk away. A minute later, she heard the bedroom door close.

Mona Lou whined and edged closer, as if the tension between the humans had upset her. Tessa clucked her tongue to soothe her and stroked her back. The dog flopped down, half in her lap. Tessa started to push her off, to go to him.

But no. They were in pretty close quarters here while they waited out the storm. A little time alone was a good thing now and then. A little space to himself, to get past whatever frightening emotions all her so-helpful suggestions had aroused.

She watched the rest of the news, tuning in and out of it, hoping the man in the other room was all right.

A half an hour after he vanished into the bedroom, she switched off the TV. By then, she was getting pretty worried. Had he passed out again? Should she go in there and make sure he was okay?

Something held her back from that. All day, he'd seemed fine. Well, except for the wound on his head and all the bruises on his body. And the memory he didn't have.

Sheesh. When she added up his injuries and the whole amnesia thing, it started to seem irresponsible of her to let him go in the bedroom and stay there, with the door closed. Still, she couldn't go barging in on him constantly, every time he wanted a few minutes to himself. That would get old really fast.

To avoid looking in on him for a little longer, she took Mona down for some outside time.

When she started back up again, the door at the top of the stairs was open and he was waiting in the doorway. She paused on the third step, Mona behind her.

He said, "I'm a jerk."

Mona waddled past her, going on up. He stepped aside so the dog could get by.

He asked, "So are you not speaking to me?"

She stared up at him, thinking what a gorgeous man he was, wishing she had the answers for him, doubting the wisdom of this thing between them, this powerful attraction.

This amazing, out-of-nowhere love affair.

"Tessa. Please."

She lowered her head and stared blindly at her shoes, wondering where they were going, how it would all turn out. Finally, she looked up at him again. "No, you're not a jerk. And yes, I am speaking to you."

"I got a little…freaked over the whole thing."

"Perfectly understandable."

"Yeah. But then I took it out on you. That *wasn't* understandable. Or even acceptable. And I'm sorry. Please forgive me."

She sent him a slow smile. "I'll think about it."

His eyes grew darker. Softer. "Come up here."

"Oh, I get it. Now you want to kiss and make up, do you?"

"That's right. I want to show you just how sorry I am."

Her body warmed at the low, tempting sound of his voice. She took one step up—and hesitated.

He put his hand down. "Don't stop now."

She ascended the rest of the way. Into his waiting arms.

Deep in the night, he woke.

Tessa slept deeply beside him, her breathing even and shallow. The cat was at his feet, the dog at hers.

He lay very still, staring up into the darkness, taking stock. His head was hurting again—not the ice-pick stabbing kind of hurt, but the dull, throbbing ache.

He'd been dreaming, fractured dreams that changed as quickly as they took form. And this time, he remembered snatches of what he'd dreamed.

In one dream, he sat at a wide desk in a corner office. A young woman entered. She had chestnut hair and blue eyes that sparkled with mischief and life.

"Zoe," he said. *"You can't just barge in here. Melody should have stopped you."*

"She tried. I gave her a big smile and a wave and walked right on by. Come on. I'm taking you to lunch."

"I'm working."

Zoe wrinkled up her nose at him. "You're my big brother, Ash, and I love you. But you work too much...."

The office vanished.

He sat by a campfire, at night. He wore a western hat,

tipped low on his forehead. He looked down his legs, clad in faded denim, at dusty rawhide boots. The fire was warm on his face, shooting up sparks into the star-thick sky. In the distance, he heard the cry of a coyote.

There were others with him. Men. Six men. Dressed as he was, in faded jeans, western shirts and dusty boots, each around his age or younger. He glanced from face to face. Each was familiar, each looked a little like the face he saw when he looked in the mirror.

"Just like old times," one of the men said. "We should do this more often."

Another laughed. "Not real likely. And when you think about it, that's damn sad."

Another, stretched out across the campfire, asked him, "Pass me a beer, will you, Ash?"

And then he was in a ballroom—red and gold, giant crystal chandeliers shimmering overhead. He looked down and he was wearing a tux, his shoes shiny black on a white marble floor. Someone tapped him on the shoulder, a woman—he knew that because he smelled her expensive, musky perfume. And then she spoke, her voice low and intimate, in his ear.

"There you are, darling. I've been looking all over for you."

Dread curled through him, tightening like a noose. He knew he would have to turn and deal with her.

Chapter Nine

Did he turn and face the woman in the ballroom?

He couldn't remember. That part was lost to him. The dream had changed again, hadn't it? It became…

He didn't know.

He lay on his back next to Tessa, listening to the gentle rhythm of her breathing, and couldn't recall what the dream became, couldn't remember the rest. But at least he'd kept some of it this time: the corner office, the sister named Zoe. The ballroom and the woman who called him darling, the woman he didn't want to deal with.

And the name. *His* name. Ash.

So Tessa had been right. Apparently his name was Ash. The gray, powdery stuff left over after everything burned to the ground. That was him. Ash.

Beside him, Tessa stirred. The bed shifted as she rolled

to her side, facing him. Her sleepy voice came to him, sweet as poured honey. "Bill?"

He turned on his side, too. Under the blankets, he ran a hand along the smooth skin of her outer arm. "I'm right here." He could have corrected her, told her he knew his name now and it was Ash, just as she'd tried to tell him before.

But no. For now, at least, he preferred Bill. It was a good name. Simple. Uncomplicated. Clear.

Her toe touched his leg, a teasing caress. He felt her hand on the side of his face.

"I'm so glad," she whispered.

He felt a smile lift the corners of his mouth. "That I'm here?"

"Uh-huh. Glad to wake up and find you beside me." She turned to her other side and wiggled backward until she was snuggled in against him, spoon-fashion.

Content in a way he knew now he'd never been before, he curled an arm around her waist and tucked her in closer, wrapping her in the warmth of his body.

The next time Ash woke, he was on his other side, facing the nightstand and the clock. It was 8:32 a.m. The glowing digital numerals meant the power remained on.

He got up and opened the curtains. Gray daylight again. The snow was still coming down, but not nearly as heavily as before. The wind had died down.

From the bed, Tessa yawned and stretched. "I'll check the phone…." She scooted over to the side of the bed he'd left vacant and grabbed the extension there. "Still out." She set it down with a sigh.

Ash tried not to feel relief. The snow piled up so high

on the sill and the phone out of order meant more stolen, intimate hours he would have with her.

They showered together, which led to lovemaking. Then they had breakfast, let the dog out, brought the dog back in.

And went back to bed to make love some more.

Outside, by late morning, the snow had stopped falling. They watched the local news at noon. Still nothing about a man going missing near Highway 49. But they did learn that the storm had officially passed. Road crews were out and on the job, clearing the highway.

"They'll be plowing the side roads by tomorrow morning, I'll bet," Tessa said. "And that means we'll most likely be able to get out by tomorrow afternoon."

"Great." He made an effort to sound enthusiastic. It *was* a good thing, to get out, to try and get more answers than a few disjointed dreams had given him.

But already he felt a heaviness inside himself, a kind of mourning for the private world they'd made, just the two of them, alone in her house, with hours and hours of time together. With no interruptions from the world outside.

That night, in bed, he asked for more stories about her family. She told him about her uncles, Jared and Brendan. Both of them were happily married, with kids. Jared's wife, Eden, ran The Hole in the Wall Saloon and The Mercantile Grill next door to it.

"Hold on a minute," he said. "You said your grandpa and grandma had *three* sons."

"And they did. Jared, my dad and Brendan."

"What about Jack? He's on your mother's side?"

"No. Uncle Jack wasn't Grandma Bathsheba's. He's Grandpa Oggie's son, from before my grandpa met my grandma. And Jack's last name is Roper, his stepfather's name. Uncle Jack married an heiress, Olivia Larrabee. He was a private investigator at the time and her rich daddy hired him to keep an eye on her when she busted loose from her father's control and decided to live life on her own. She came here to North Magdalene totally by accident. And Uncle Jack was on her trail. Turned out she'd led him to the home of the father he never knew he had."

Ash groaned. "Come on, Tessa."

"What? God's truth. It happened just that way."

"It's a little far-fetched, that she would come here with no clue it was where his long-lost natural father lived. It's too coincidental."

"What can I tell you? Life. Stranger than fiction and that is no lie."

They'd left the curtains open and the half moon shone through the cloud cover, giving her skin a silvery glow, leaching the gold from her hair so it shone platinum across the pillow.

"I never want to leave here," he confessed in a whisper. "I want to stay here with you, like this, forever."

The window was behind her, casting her face in shadow, so he couldn't read her expression. He heard her soft sigh. She didn't reply, only found his hand under the blankets and twined her fingers tight with his.

He woke in the morning to the sound of an engine—roaring and then fading off a little, laboring nearer.

Tessa popped to a sitting position, clutching the sheet against her breasts, shoving her hair back out of her eyes. "Do you hear that?" At his nod, she crowed, "It's the snowplow and it's coming up my driveway!"

They got dressed fast and went out to wave at the plow driver, who honked his horn and gave them an answering wave.

Ash felt vaguely ridiculous in his borrowed purple sweats and smooth-soled boots as the driver plowed forward, reversed, and plowed forward again, gradually forming a turnaround, until he was headed back the way he'd come. With a final wave, he drove off down the freshly cleared road to the highway, disappearing into the trees.

Tessa turned to him, beaming. "We are out of here today." They went inside and she checked the phone. "Nothing yet." She put it back in its cradle.

They ate a quick breakfast and then went out with shovels to clear the short path to her Subaru. With no other shoes around that fit him, Ash had to do his shoveling in the slick-soled boots he'd arrived in. He slipped a lot as they worked. But the activity was bracing, after being housebound for three days. His headache was long-gone and his body was healing already from the mysterious battering it had taken.

He felt good. Strong. More or less ready to take on the big world out there.

It took about forty-five minutes of heavy shoveling, but they got the path cleared to the driveway. By then, they were both panting, breathless from the job. Tessa's nose and cheeks were red. And her lips, too. He watched her, thinking that he'd like to be kissing her.

And what about a snowball fight? That could be fun.

When she bent to scoop up a last shovelful, he grabbed a handful of the cold white stuff and held it out of sight at his side.

"Tessa?"

The shovel scraped concrete, and she threw that final shovelful out of the way. "Whew." She leaned on the handle, her breath pluming in the air. "Hmm?"

He stepped up, grabbed the collar of her purple jacket and dropped the snow down her back.

She let out a shriek. "Oh, you! I'll get you…" Her shovel clattered to the frozen driveway as she bent to grab a big mittenful of snow.

He let go of his shovel, too, put up both hands and backed the way they had come, slipping on the icy ground a little, but managing to stay on his feet. "Now, Tessa. Be calm…"

With another shriek, she fired the snowball. It hit him square in the jaw.

He wiped it away. "You shouldn't have done that."

"Oh, yeah. I should."

"You are going to be so, so sorry…"

She laughed. "Hah!" Grabbing snow, forming another ball of ammunition, she backed away.

And he came toward her, grabbing his own snowball. They fired simultaneously. He hit her in the nose. She got him on the cheekbone.

With a cry, she turned and started for the driveway. He gave chase, forgetting that his boots weren't made for running on ice. He slipped. And then went down, legs out, landing on his backside.

She turned and saw him and started to laugh.

"That's it," he growled. "Wait till I get up from here. You will pay, Tessa Jones. You will pay…."

Still laughing, she came to him and held down a hand. "Come on. Be nice. Forgive and forget."

He reached up, took hold—and pulled her down on top of him.

She shrieked again in surprise and punched him in the shoulder. "That's what I get for trying to help you."

He let his head rest on the cold concrete. "It's nice here."

She rolled her eyes at him. "Oh, yeah. Flat on your back on a frozen driveway."

"Don't complain. *You* have me between you and the concrete."

"True." Those light-hazel eyes twinkled. "Being on top never felt better."

"Down here, though, I'm really starting to feel the cold."

"So let's get up."

He banded an arm around her, holding her down. "A kiss first. That would really warm me up."

She shook her head. And then she giggled. And then she lowered her mouth to his.

Her lips were cold. But they quickly turned warm. And beyond them, she was hot and slick and wet as ever. He could have lain there for decades, kissing her.

But then she lifted her head. "Come on. I mean it. We need to get up before that fine backside of yours freezes solid."

Reluctantly, he released her. She rose and held down a hand again. He took it and she helped him rise. They were just turning for the house when they heard tires crunching gravel and the rough rumble of an engine. A battered, old pickup was turning into the driveway.

Tessa turned toward the sound. "Wouldn't you know it?"

"Who is it?"

"My grandfather, Oggie Jones."

The pickup came to a stop a few feet from where they stood. The ancient character inside rolled down the crank window. "Hey there, Tessy. How you holdin' up?"

"Tessa," she corrected. "And Grandpa, I'm fine. Just fine."

The old guy grunted. "Well, Tessy. You'll be pleased to know that everyone else in the family is A-Okay, too."

"I'm sure you've checked on all of them." Ash noticed she didn't correct the old man again for calling her Tessy. There was probably no point in it. Oggie Jones didn't seem the kind who responded to correction.

"Yes, I have checked on everyone. Closer in, the phones are back on, but when I tried your number, it was still out."

"I'm sure it'll come on soon."

"I thought I better come on over and make sure about you, just the same."

"Thanks—but really, everything's okay."

Oggie stuck a chewed-looking cigar stub between his teeth and poked his arm out the window to give the truck door a whack. "Can't believe how bad the road is. Couldn't get my El Dorado out of the driveway. Had to fire up the old pickup." He gunned the engine, which sputtered and then roared as he squinted in Ash's direction. Eventually, he took his foot off the gas. His wrinkled forehead beetled up. "This that boyfriend of yours from Napa?"

Ash stepped up before Tessa could reveal more than he wanted known. "Bill," he said firmly. "How're you doing?" He pulled off the work glove Tessa had loaned him and offered his hand.

The old guy grabbed it and gave it a good pump. "Well, what d'you know? The man from Napa makes an appearance at last." He took the smashed stub of cigar from the corner of his mouth and gave the nonexistent ash a flick. "You ain't exactly what I expected, if you don't mind my sayin'. 'Cept for the purple sweatpants. They seem about right."

"Grandpa!" Tessa was blushing. "Be nice."

"I'm always nice." The old guy had a few wisps of wiry white fringe above his ears. The rest of his head was shiny as a bowling ball. His heavy, worn-looking green jacket was open. Ash caught a glimpse of a grimy flannel shirt and red suspenders. "What'd you do to your head?"

"I tripped and fell."

"Ah," the old man replied. "Gotta be more careful."

"You're right. I will."

"Tessy here's the nicest of all my grandkids," the old man announced. "Such a sweet gal. She wanted to be a nun when she was a girl. Glad she gave that up. Bet you are, too." He wiggled his bushy brows.

"I am. Real glad." Ash put an arm around Tessa, who looked like she couldn't wait for her grandfather to turn his old pickup around and head back the way he'd come.

The old man kept talking. "Naw, Tessy ain't nun material. Tessy's strong and capable. And would you look at those hips? She was made for the hot, sweet lovin' of a good man, meant to raise a passel of fine children...."

"Grandpa," said Tessa much too pleasantly. "You talk too much."

Oggie didn't argue the point. "Always have, always will." *Passel?* Ash was thinking. Did people still say words like *passel?* "And how come we're all hanging around out here in the cold? Let's go on inside. You can fix me up a cup of hot coffee to warm these old bones."

Tessa was frowning again. "Grandpa, I'm sorry, but right now we're in kind of a hurry." Ash knew what came next: all about how they were headed over to the clinic to see what could be done about the problem with his brain.

He caught her hand—and cut her off. "Coffee," he said firmly. "Tessa. Your grandfather came all the way over here. We can certainly have him in and give him some coffee."

"But…Bill." She threw him a look he was careful not to catch. "You know that we really should get to the—"

"Coffee," declared Oggie. "Won't take but a few minutes." The pickup's door swung wide with a rusty squeak. The old man reached for a cane propped up on the passenger seat and swung himself out and down to the slippery ground. "Give me a hand here, you two. I ain't as steady on my feet as I used to be."

Inside, there was coffee left from breakfast—still hot, too. With the power restored, Tessa had gone back to using an electric coffee maker. Oggie hobbled to the table and pulled out a chair. He propped his cane close at hand, but kept his jacket on. "Lots of sugar, Tessy."

"I know, I know." She put a full mug in front of him and slid the sugar close as Ash grabbed a chair.

Oggie spooned in half the contents of the sugar bowl and slurped up a big sip. "Ah. That's good. That's real good." He swung his rheumy gaze Ash's way. "So. You drove up from the wine country Saturday, did you?"

"Yeah. Lucky for me, I made it before the snow got too bad."

"Where's your car? Don't see it out there…" Oggie peered out the window as if expecting the missing vehicle to materialize from thin air.

Ash shared a glance with Tessa. She started to speak.

He beat her to it. "I got some time off work. But my car's been acting up. Lucky for me, a friend of mine was coming this way. He dropped me off Saturday before noon."

"Made it just before the storm closed in, eh?"

"Lucky for me, huh?"

"So how long you here for?"

"It's…open-ended."

"But you're staying for the wedding, right?"

Ash remembered: the wedding that the *real* Bill had promised to attend with Tessa. "That's right. I'll be here for Tawny and Parker's wedding. Really looking forward to that."

The old man gave a cackle. "Oh, I'll just bet." He turned to Tessa, who leaned against the sink counter, arms crossed over her chest. "Good coffee, Tessy." He saluted her with the mug.

She leveled a look on him that said his welcome was swiftly wearing out. "Enjoy."

He winked at Ash. "She gets fed up with me. They all get fed up with me. But they love me, just the same. I'm one of a kind, you just ask anyone."

"I can see that," said Ash.

The old man leaned a forearm on the table and canted toward Ash. "So, Bill. How old you think I am? Go ahead, take a guess."

Tessa let out a heavy sigh. "Grandpa, just tell him, why don't you?"

Oggie ignored her. "Go on. Guess."

Old, Ash thought. Really, really old. "Eighty-five?"

The old man crowed in delight and pounded a hand on the tabletop. "Ninety-one. And still going strong—so how d'you like our beautiful mountains?"

"A lot. I like them a lot."

"Tessy should take you out hiking if it warms up a little and the snow melts down some. Nothin' like a long hike up into the high elevations to get the blood pumping and the attitude adjusted."

Ash nodded. "We'll have to do that. Won't we, Tessa?"

Tessa folded her arms even tighter. "Yeah. Great idea."

The old man drained his mug and set it down hard. "All right, all right. I know you got a million things you need to be doing." He grabbed for his cane and pushed himself upright. "Good to meet you, Bill."

"Same here, Oggie."

"You treat my Tessy right."

"I will."

"And take my advice."

"Sure."

"Don't go wearing those purple sweatpants around town."

They helped Tessa's grandfather back out to the pickup and stood waving as he drove away.

She turned to him once the old truck rumbled from sight. "I thought he'd never go. Just let me grab my purse and keys and we'll get over to the clinic."

He put his hand on her arm. "The old man was right. I can't go running around in women's sweats."

She gave him a tender smile. "Men. Really, don't worry. We'll deal with the clothing issue. But the clinic comes first."

He released her and stepped back. "I feel fine."

She gaped at him. "Maybe you do feel fine now. But you were comatose for hours."

"That was Saturday. I've been conscious—except for normal sleep—ever since."

She pressed her lips together. He knew she was reminding herself to go easy on him. "You're suffering from amnesia, remember?"

He glared at her. "As if it's something I could forget."

"You have headaches."

"Hardly at all the past couple of days—and let's go inside. We don't need to stand out here and freeze while we argue over this." He turned and headed for the house. She didn't follow. He glanced back at her. "Come inside. Please."

Her mouth a grim line, she finally started walking.

Inside, he hung the coat she'd loaned him on the hook in the front hall. She kept hers on—and her snow boots, too, a decision that did not bode well for his chances of convincing her to forget about the clinic visit. She was ready to go and staying that way.

He went in and took a seat at the table. She remained standing at the counter, in about the same spot she'd stood while she waited for her grandfather to leave.

She said, tightly, "Are you telling me that you refuse to get medical help? Because I'm so serious here, Bill. You *need,* at the very least, to let someone who knows about brain injuries have a look at you."

"And then what?"

"What do you mean?"

"After they have a look at me, then what?"

"Well, I don't know. Will Bacon—he's the nurse-practitioner at the clinic—will decide what's next. Maybe a CAT scan, or X-rays, or whatever. Maybe surgery. Maybe…honestly, Bill. I don't know. If I knew, I'd be a doctor. And I'm not."

He didn't want it. He *really* didn't want some doctor or nurse working him over, asking him questions when he had no answers. Or cutting his head open, if it came to that. The idea made his skin crawl. Plus, somehow, deep down, he knew it would all be unnecessary.

He *knew* he was getting better. He hadn't had a headache since the other night when he dreamed of his real life—and actually remembered a little of it. He improved daily.

Hourly. Every damn minute. He was going to be fine in the end. He'd recover on his own, he was absolutely sure of that. All he really needed was time. His memory, already returning in snatches, would eventually come back completely.

But she looked so damned determined.

In the end, Ash knew she would find a way to make him do what she felt was right for him. "Okay."

Her sweet face lit up. "You'll go?"

"I'll go."

"Now?"

"Yeah," he agreed, even though he could think of a thousand good reasons not to.

Who the hell was going to pay for it? They'd have to take a damn IOU. Tessa was already footing the tab for his daily existence. Damned if he'd let her take responsibility for his medical bills, too.

And how would he fill out his personal information when he didn't have any? Not to mention, what about his medical history? He didn't have that, either. He had no history of any kind before Saturday—well, beyond knowing his name was Asher, called Ash, and a few random details about a large family that had to be out there somewhere, along with some unknown woman he dreaded having to face....

Tessa snatched her keys from the key rack and her purse from its spot at the end of the counter. "Let's go, then." She headed for the door.

Resigned to his fate, Ash got up and followed her out.

Chapter Ten

"I can't believe this," Tessa fumed.

The local clinic had been set up in what Ash assumed had once been someone's house—a cute, yellow clapboard cottage with white shutters. They stood on the front porch.

The place was locked up tight. A note taped to the door said the clinic was temporarily closed. *For further information, call 555-3695.*

Ash tried not to look as relieved as he felt to be let off this particular hook. "Not a big deal," he said mildly. "I'm fine, really."

The dark, determined glance she shot him made it all too clear that she hadn't given up on getting him the medical attention she was so sure he needed. "Come on. We'll see if the phone's working at the store."

So they got back in the wagon and she drove them to Main Street. She parked in the lot by the town hall and they crossed the street to a shop between the gold sales store and the café. Jones Mercantile, the sign read in old-timey letters that matched the ones on the signs at the bar across and down the street and The Mercantile Grill next to it.

A couple of elderly women—one skinny, the other built like a tank—tromped up in snow boots, baggy jeans and fat down jackets as Tessa unlocked the glass-topped door.

"Nellie. Linda Lou." Tessa smiled and nodded.

"Teresa," said the skinny one, with a sharp look for Ash—including a definite scowl when she took in the purple sweats.

"My friend, Bill," Tessa said. Ash knew a moment's gratitude that she'd tacitly agreed to carry on with the fiction that he was someone he wasn't. It just made things simpler, for now. And kept people from asking a lot of un-answerable questions. These two, he could tell at first glance, would consider it their civic duty to find out everything they could about him. "Bill, this is Linda Lou Beardsly." Tessa tipped her head at the big one. "And Nellie Anderson." A smile in the skinny one's direction.

"Pleased to meet you, ladies."

The two nodded and gave him a grudging, "Hello," in unison. The skinny one said, "What happened to your head?"

He gave her a half shrug. "Ran into a door."

The big one asked, "So you're Tessa's special friend from Napa, are you? I've been wondering when you'd finally show up."

As Ash tried to decide how to reply to that one, Tessa dealt with it. "Well, he's here now and I'm so glad." She gave him a fond smile.

The two old ladies exchanged knowing looks.

"Are you opening up?" Nellie, the skinny one, wanted to know.

"Not today," Tessa told her. "Got some things to… catch up on first. But tomorrow at ten for sure. Unless there's something you need right now?"

"No," said the big one. "Not a thing. Nellie?"

"I was only curious, that's all. I hate to walk around town and see half the businesses dark. These storms are just so disruptive." Nellie pursed up her skinny lips and shook her head in disapproval—as if the weather ought to pay attention to her complaint and do better next time.

"We'll be back to normal by tomorrow," Tessa promised with a bright smile. "See you two later." She pushed the door open.

The two got the message and trudged on by at last.

Inside, Tessa punched some buttons on a simple alarm and then went around turning on lights. Ash hung back as she disappeared through another door on the far side of the large main room.

He glanced around. The store was wood-floored and wood-paneled, with a pressed-tin ceiling maybe twenty feet up. His first impression was that Jones Mercantile was the small-town version of a department store. At the far wall, above the door to the back room, stairs ascended to an open second floor. He could see clothing up there. Downstairs was for housewares, jewelry, towels and sheets, all kinds of knickknacks, pictures, scented soaps, stuff women went gaga for. He guessed Tessa did a good business with the locals and with whatever tourist trade the town attracted.

She came back through the door. He heard a heater kick in. "Warm things up in here," she said with a shiver.

"Teresa?" he repeated the name Nellie Anderson had called her. "Is that your given name?"

"Unfortunately."

"You don't like it."

"I hate it. When we were kids and Marnie and I were always fighting, she started calling me Saint Teresa—partly because of the whole nun thing my grandpa mentioned and also because I was such a goody-goody type. Most of the kids in town picked it up."

"And what about 'Tessy'?"

"That was my nickname, too. I never liked it, not anymore than I liked being called Saint Teresa. When I was in my teens, I started insisting my name was Tessa. I refused to answer to anything else. Eventually, everyone accepted that I was Tessa now. Well, except for my grandpa. Nobody tells Oggie Jones what to do."

He grinned. "How long have you owned this place?"

"Five years. It used be a barber shop and variety store owned by the Santino family. But when they decided to sell out, my dad and Gina helped me buy it. Come on." She signaled him back through the door with her, into a storage area and on through another door into a small, windowless office. She sat at the tidy oak desk, dropped her keys and her purse, and snatched up the phone. "Bingo." She smiled wide. "We're in business. I'll just give the clinic a call, see what's up." She dialed and then signaled him to take the one extra chair.

He felt too edgy at the looming prospect of medical treatment to sit, so he lurked in the doorway. She listened. "Great," she muttered, meaning it wasn't. She scribbled a number on her desk pad and hung up. "The answering machine at the clinic says they're closed until next week.

Will Bacon—that's the nurse practitioner—is out of town till a week from tomorrow. If there's an emergency while he's gone, we're supposed to call Sierra Nevada Memorial in Grass Valley. Which is pointless." Pointless. Was that good news? Was she finally giving this up? She went on, "I mean, why call? We might as well just go on down there."

"Down…?"

"To Grass Valley. It's less than an hour away." She grabbed her keys and purse again and shoved back her chair. "Let's get moving."

He just didn't want to do it. "Enough." She was halfway around the desk. He went to her, took her by the shoulders and guided her backward.

"Stop this." She tried to shrug him off. "We have to—"

"No." Gently he pushed her back into the chair. "We don't."

"We do." When she tried to rise again, he grabbed on to the chair arms and trapped her there.

He also pinned her with his determined gaze. "Accept it. The crisis has passed. Whatever happened to me, I'm getting better. I'll recover completely in time. Watch me."

"But you still need to—"

"Tessa. I'm not going to the damn hospital."

"You are. You have to."

"I'm not. And I don't."

A stare-down ensued. He refused to give in. She was the one who dropped her gaze first. "I'll never forgive myself if anything happens to you."

He touched her chin, urging her to look at him. When she finally met his gaze, he said, "Nothing is going to happen. And if it did—which it won't—it wouldn't be your fault anyway. It would be mine. I'm making this decision, not you."

"But—"

He didn't let her finish. "I'll say it again. I'm not going."

"I just…" She was weakening, realizing that if he flat-out refused to go, there wasn't much she could do about it. "You have to face reality here. You don't even know who you are. You need medical help, Bill."

"Ash," he corrected her softly, knowing he had to give her something in the way of proof he was getting better. "My name is Ash."

She gaped at him. Wonder filled those gold-green eyes. "You've…remembered?"

He nodded.

"But…you didn't say a word."

"Yeah, well. I should have, I guess."

She reached up, cupped his face between her hands. "Oh, you'd better believe you should have."

"I don't remember everything," he warned. "Really, it's not much. But I feel…encouraged, you know?"

"Tell me. All of it."

So he sat on the edge of her desk and filled her in on the things he'd recalled about his family and about the life he'd lived before he came to her. He left out the mysterious woman in the ballroom, telling himself he'd wait on that. Until he saw the woman's face. Until he knew who she was and what significance she had to him.

"It's something," he said, when he was finished. "But I could really use a last name. Maybe a phone number or a mailing address. I have this feeling I'm from Texas. Though I'm not sure why I think that."

"Texas, huh? Well, this is definitely a start. I'm so glad—and I still think you should see a doctor."

He only looked at her. Steadily.

She blew out a breath. "Will you at least promise that if the headaches come back, if you have blurry vision or feel nauseous or anything like that, you'll tell me and we'll head straight for the hospital?"

"Deal."

"I don't like it."

"You've made that more than clear."

She stood again. "All right then. Time to go visit my Uncle Jack."

Damn. The sheriff. He still had that to get through.

"I don't like your expression," she muttered. "Don't try and tell me we're not going to talk to Uncle Jack."

"Look. I'm willing to go see him, to tell him all I know…."

"Why am I hearing a 'but' in there somewhere?"

"I just want your agreement that the sheriff is one thing. But for everyone else around here, let me keep on being Bill. It's a lot easier than trying to explain the truth. Everyone's heard of your boyfriend, Bill, right?"

She rolled her eyes. "Unfortunately, yes."

"So if I'm Bill, it cuts down on the questions."

She gave him one of those so-patient looks of hers. "It's obvious you know nothing about the people in this town. There will be questions no matter what you call yourself."

"But fewer, if I'm Bill."

"No. Really. The more I think about this, the more certain I am that lying is only going to create more problems than it can possibly solve. You say you're certain your memory will return in full."

"Yeah. So?"

"So, when you remember everything, when you know who you are completely, *then* what will we tell them? That I *thought* you were the Bill I met in Napa, but I was mistaken?"

What she said made way too much sense.

But he still felt protective, somehow, of all he didn't know about his "real" self. He preferred making up a temporary identity to admitting outright that he didn't know who he was.

He muttered defensively, "We're already set with Bill."

"Says who?"

"I introduced myself as Bill to your grandfather. And then there were those two ladies we saw on the street. They think I'm Bill, too."

"So?" Now she was the one rising, taking *him* by the shoulders. "Tell them the truth the next time you see them. Just, you know, 'Sorry for the confusion. My name is Asher. Call me Ash.' You don't need to explain. No matter what they hit you with, shrug and move on. You don't owe them any explanations. And what's the point in lying, really? It'll only trip you up in the end. Plus, when you finally remember everything and get your real identity back, you'll just have more explaining to do. Better to be honest, but vague, at this point."

He knew she was right. In the end, there *was* no protecting himself from questions he couldn't answer. Maybe he needed to stop trying to hide from everything he didn't know.

"All right," he said, and discovered the choice to be honest had him feeling more at ease in his own skin than he had since he found himself riding down the highway in a big rig with no clue who he was or how he got there. "Ash, then. Call me Ash."

"Ash." She said it softly. "It's a beautiful name. I really love it." And then she bent closer. She kissed him, a tender press of her lips to his. Before he got a chance to wrap her tight in his arms and ramp up the heat a little, she was pulling away. "Okay. Now, for the sheriff's station…"

"One more thing."

She braced her hands on her hips. "Isn't there always?"

He grabbed a handful of purple sweats. "Do you sell men's clothing in here?"

She looked relieved. "Now, *that* I can help you with."

Forty-five minutes later, dressed in jeans and sturdy lace-up boots, a black sweatshirt and a new jacket, Ash shook hands with Jack Roper. Tessa's uncle was tanned and fit in middle age, his piercing black eyes a startling contrast to his almost-white hair.

"Ash…?" Roper was waiting for a last name.

Ash shrugged. "Can't say—which is a big part of what we came to see you about."

Roper frowned. "I think maybe we need a little privacy. This way." He gestured them into the back, where he led them to his office and shut the door. "Have a seat." Ash and Tessa sat opposite the desk. Roper offered coffee, which they declined. He went around and took the desk chair.

After a minute or two of small talk about the storm and how everyone seemed to have made it through in one piece, he asked, "So then, Ash. Why can't you say what your last name is?"

"Because I don't know." As simply and directly as he could, Ash told the sheriff all he knew. From the truck ride down the mountain to the way Tessa had rescued him and cared for him while they waited out the storm. He said what he'd remembered of who he was—except for the unknown woman in the ballroom. He kept that to himself.

When he'd finished, the first question out of the sheriff's mouth was, "That gash on your forehead looks nasty. Have you been to a doctor?"

Tessa piped up. "He won't go."

Roper looked at him as if he'd lost more than his memory. "Go. Let them at least do a physical exam. A wound like you've got there is nothing to fool with, not with the symptoms you just described—plus, if it turns out a crime has been committed, we'll be in better shape to do something about it if you've seen a doctor and there's a medical record of your injuries and whatever treatment you underwent."

Ash glanced at Tessa. At least she had the grace not to look smug. He felt pretty damn foolish. In the end, there was no way to escape a trip to the hospital in Grass Valley. Denial wasn't going to help him get past whatever had happened to him. He would have to submit to an exam, at least.

Submit. Interesting word choice. And probably another clue to his original self. In his previous life, he'd lay odds he hadn't been much for submitting to anything. He had a sense of his other self as a man with power. A man in control. It fit with the big corner office he'd dreamed of, and the little sister who said he worked too much.

"Fine," he told the sheriff. "I give in. As soon as we're through here, we'll go to Grass Valley and visit the hospital." Tessa caught his hand, gave it a squeeze. They shared a warm glance. When Ash faced the sheriff again, the dark eyes were watching, taking everything in.

"Good." Roper scribbled something on the notepad in front of him. "And for now, you're staying with Tessa. Is that right?"

"Yes." Tessa was the one who answered that one, her chin high and her voice firm. "Ash is staying at my place. You can reach him there."

Roper nodded, wrote something else on the pad. "Anything else you can think of? Anything that comes to mind, no matter how seemingly irrelevant to your situation. You never know the off-the-wall stuff that might provide us with a lead."

Tessa said, "There was one thing. When he first showed up at my house before the storm and passed out in the snow, I noticed he smelled really strongly of alcohol."

As she said it, Ash remembered the same thing. "That's right. During the ride down the mountain in that semi-truck, I remember wondering why I reeked of booze."

Tessa said, "It was all over his clothes, but I don't think he was drunk. There was no alcohol on his breath."

Roper made more notes. "Anything else?"

Ash shook his head. "We've been watching the news, but there's been nothing that might tell us who I really am or how I got here."

Roper made a low noise in his throat. "I'll look into it from a few different angles and get back to you as soon as I learn anything. And another option…"

Tessa leaned forward. "What? Tell us."

"You'll be in the local paper, *The North Magdalene News,* next Tuesday…."

Ash frowned at Tessa. "I will?"

"The Sheriff's Blotter, right?" she asked her uncle.

"Right." Roper explained, "It's a weekly feature in the *News,* a community service. Lets people know what's going on in local law enforcement—and in a case like yours, it gets the word out about you. Someone might step forward with information that could help you. And you *could* take it farther."

"How?" Ash asked even though he wasn't sure he wanted to know.

"You could contact the daily newspapers with wider circulation, the *Grass Valley Union,* the *Bee* down in Sacramento. You might even try one of the Sacramento TV stations. You get them interested, get a story out statewide or beyond, you multiply your chances that someone will recognize you."

Tessa lit up. "That's a great idea."

Ash could just see the headline: *Man without a Memory Found Wandering in the Sierras.* Made him feel like some freak show attraction. But if it had to be done, so be it.

Roper asked, in an offhanded tone, "Will you consent to be fingerprinted?"

Ash instantly recognized the question for what it was. A test. If he said yes, the sheriff's office would check his prints against some giant national database packed full of the prints of people who'd had run-ins with the law.

Am I a criminal?

It would be one explanation for the way he seemed to have appeared out of thin air. An escape of some kind into the Sierras, maybe. And then the incident that had battered his body and cost him his memory...

No. It didn't feel right. It didn't fit with what he'd recalled of his past so far.

Or maybe I just don't want to believe it fits.

The sheriff was waiting. Watching.

Asher realized the choice had been made when he let Tessa drag him in there. "Whatever it takes. Sure. I'll be fingerprinted."

Tessa was pleased with the way things were going.

Ash had not only come with her to the sheriff's station and agreed to let her Uncle Jack help him, but he'd also finally accepted the necessity of seeing a doctor. She felt so much better about everything. He'd get whatever medical care he needed—and her uncle would do everything in his power as sheriff to solve the mystery of Ash's identity and reunite him with his loved ones, who were probably worried sick about now.

Once Uncle Jack was through asking questions, he led Ash and Tessa back up front.

"I'm glad you came to me," Jack said. "And, if you remember more, if anything comes to you—anything at all—give me a call." He pressed a business card into Ash's hand. Jack caught the eye of the woman at the front desk. "Nelda? Ash here has agreed to be fingerprinted."

Nelda Bass clerked at the station and also worked as a fill-in dispatcher. She looked a lot more than curious as to what was going on. But all she said was, "Sure enough." Tessa was glad she kept her questions to herself.

"There'll be some paperwork," Jack said. "A simple consent form. Just sign your first name, since that's all you've got at this point."

Ash shrugged. "Let's get it over with."

"This way," said Nelda.

Ash turned to follow her.

"And, Tessa." Her uncle wrapped an arm across her shoulders as soon as Ash was out of sight and turned her around the way they'd come. "While Ash is busy, come on back to my office for a minute, will you?"

"But I don't—"

"Only a minute." He guided her back down the hall.

In his office, he shut the door and gestured at the chair she'd sat in before.

"I'll stand, thanks." She noticed that he didn't sit, either. Apprehension tightened the muscles between her shoulder blades and made her stomach churn. So much for feeling great about everything. "What's up?"

"Tessa…" Her uncle didn't seem to know what to say next. He hung his head and rubbed the back of his neck.

"Uncle Jack. You're making me nervous. What is going on?"

He looked at her, then, through those dark eyes that were every bit as sharp and knowing as her grandpa's. "I have a suggestion."

"Um. Okay."

"Why don't you let me take care of Ash?"

What was he telling her? "Take care of him? I don't—?"

"We don't know who he really is or where he came from, right?"

"Right. So?"

"So, we need to be realistic about this. Now that you've brought him here to the station, it's the perfect opportunity for you to let us take over."

"Us?"

"Sorry. *I'll* take over for you. I'll take total responsibility. I'll see that he's made comfortable until we can locate his family. You've done what you can for him. I think that's great. But the best thing now would be for you to let me take it from here."

Suddenly she got the picture. It wasn't a pretty one. "Oh. I get it. You think Ash might be an ax murderer or something."

"I never said—"

"Uncle Jack, you didn't *have* to say. You don't want him staying with me because you're afraid he'll hurt me in some way. Well, take my word for it. He won't."

"It's just not that simple."

"Yes, it is. And I'm the one—along with Ash—who gets to make this decision."

"Tessa, it's just not safe for you to—"

"It *is* safe. And I don't see how I can make myself any clearer. I'm not dropping Ash off with you. It's not what I want. And it's not what *he* wants."

"Tessa, you're a kind-hearted woman—"

"Stop. Just stop right there." She almost felt sorry for him. Poor Uncle Jack. Trying to find a delicate way to say that she was a total loser when it came to men, trying to tell her how he was going to save her from herself. She leveled a dead-on look at him. "I want you to listen. Carefully."

"Tessa, you're being naive about this and—"

"Uncle Jack. Would you please do me the courtesy of listening to what I have to say?"

He blew out a slow breath. "Fair enough. Talk."

"I can understand your concern. I truly can. But you have to see that if Ash was some kind of crook, he would never have agreed to come here to the station and talk to you. And he certainly wouldn't be letting Nelda take his fingerprints as we speak."

Jack rubbed the bridge of his nose between his thumb

and forefinger, the way people do when they're getting a headache. "If he has total amnesia about who he is and where he came from, the way he claims, then he has no idea whether he's a criminal or not. And if he's lying, well, you don't know the kinds of things some of these con artists will pull, you have no idea how far they'll go. You're a nice girl from North Magdalene and—"

"Enough." She said it quietly, but something in her tone must have reached him, because he did fall silent and let her talk. "Ash is telling the truth. About everything. He's no con artist. And as for me, I'm twenty-seven years old and fully capable of making my own decision about this. I've been snowed in with him since Saturday afternoon. He's been nothing but good to me. Respectful and helpful. And kind. Something terrible happened to him. But I'm not jumping to the conclusion that it's all his fault. Or that he's out to use and abuse me. I just don't believe that. I'll never believe that."

"I think you're being foolish." Her uncle spoke gently, but the words still hurt.

"Think what you want." She held her ground. "This is my decision to make and you know it is."

At last, wearily, he gave in. "Just promise you'll call me immediately if the guy does anything that scares you or gets you feeling the least uncomfortable."

"Certainly. If he scares me—which he won't—you'll be the one I call." She felt torn—angry for Ash's sake, yet also, on another level, aware that her uncle only wanted to protect her. "May I go now?"

He reached for the door and pulled it open, stepping to the side, out of her way. "Be safe. Please."

"Thank you," she told him grudgingly. "I will." She

longed to demand that he not call her dad—or, God forbid, Grandpa Oggie—about this. But she knew that her ordering him not to wouldn't change his mind. If he felt it was his duty to call her father, he would.

Foolish, he had called her. And naive. And maybe she was, though not about Ash. Her naiveté was in the way she'd dragged Ash in here, so confident she was doing the right thing for him.

She should have known her uncle wouldn't let her out of there without trying to talk her into walking away from Ash. Jack's last name might be Roper, but by blood, he was a Jones. And when her dad learned that she had a stranger with no memory living in her house?

Tessa wasn't sure what would happen.

But she had a very strong suspicion it wouldn't be good.

Chapter Eleven

When the clerk finished taking digital impressions of his fingerprints, she sent Ash out to the waiting area. Tessa wasn't there. He went to the mesh-reinforced glass doors that led to the parking spaces in front and looked out.

Her red wagon was parked where they'd left it. Apparently, she was still in the station. But where?

He no sooner thought the question than someone buzzed the door that led into the main part of the station. He turned as Tessa emerged.

She came to him wearing a forced smile. "Ready to go?"

Something had happened back there. He waited for her to tell him what. But they went out and got in the wagon and headed for Grass Valley, all without another word from her.

The highway was a twisty one, curving around mountains, winding down into canyons, over bridges that crossed deep river gorges and then winding back upward to the crest of the next the hill. Snowplows had cleared the way, but it was still frozen and potentially dangerous on most of the turns. She concentrated on her driving and Ash kept his questions to himself throughout the ride.

Eventually, they turned onto a wider highway and passed a town called Nevada City.

Tessa spoke at last. "We're almost there. Nevada City and Grass Valley are sister cities. Both started as gold-mining towns, way back when. North Magdalene, too…"

Minutes later, they were pulling into the hospital parking lot. She quickly found a space. Turning off the engine, she took the key from the ignition with another too-bright smile. "Ready?" She leaned down and grabbed her purse from near his feet.

He reached across to her door and caught her hand before she could pull on the handle.

Color bloomed up from under the high collar of her turtleneck sweater. "What?" All fluttery-eyed and innocent.

"Talk to me."

She cleared her throat. "About…?"

"Tessa. I have to tell you. You're really lousy at pretending nothing's bothering you when something is."

"I…um…"

"Come on. Give it up."

With a sad little groan, she sagged forward until her forehead met the steering wheel. He waited. He knew she would tell him eventually.

Finally, she dragged her shoulders up and sat straight in the seat. "Uncle Jack called me back to talk to me alone. He's suspicious of you."

Was he surprised? Not in the least. "So what? *I'm* suspicious of me."

She made a tight sound in her throat. "Well, *I'm* not."

"That's just…how you are."

"Foolish, you mean? And naive?"

"I didn't say that."

"You didn't have to."

"Come on. You have to see it through his eyes. Some guy without even a last name is staying with you, mooching off you. Hell. I could be an ax murderer, for all we know."

She sent him a sharp look. And then she burst out laughing.

He scowled at her. "I don't think that's especially funny."

She waved a hand. "Oh, it's just, well, that's what *I* said."

"That you thought I was an ax murderer?"

She punched him lightly on the arm. "No. That you *weren't* an ax murderer or anything like that."

"I'll bet the sheriff found *that* reassuring," he muttered drily.

"Yeah. Well. Maybe not. The point is, I told him I trusted you and that you would never do anything to harm me."

"Let me guess. He wasn't buying."

"Right."

"Tessa, he's a cop. It's his job *not* to trust strangers."

"Whatever. In the end, Uncle Jack and I agreed to disagree. And that's all, that's the whole story." She reached for the door again.

He caught her hand first. "So what's worrying you?"

"I didn't say anything was worrying me."

Ash simply stared at her. Waiting.

She opened her purse and slid her keys into a pocket inside. Then she snapped it shut. "Okay. It's just…you would have to know the men in my family. Uncle Jack will probably call my dad. And my dad's not going to like it, that you're staying with me—not after Uncle Jack gets through explaining how you don't know who you are and you could be dangerous. And when my dad doesn't like something, well, he takes action."

He caught her sweet face between his hands. "It's okay. I'll find somewhere else to stay."

"No." Her eyes were so bright. And her strong chin was set. "Don't you dare. I mean it. Don't you dare let them chase you away from me."

"They're only thinking of your welfare."

"So am I. I want you with me, Ash. For as long as this crazy, wonderful thing between us lasts. For as long as you *want* to be with me."

"But you have to consider—"

She shut him up by leaning in and kissing him. Hard. When she pulled away, she fiercely declared, "All I have to consider is do I want you with me and do *you* want to be there? I know the answer for my part of the question. I want you to stay with me. What about you?"

"Tessa..."

She surged forward and caught his mouth again in a kiss as hard and insistent as the one before. But that time, she didn't pull back right away. Instead, she sighed and her body swayed closer to him. He wrapped his arms around her and the kiss turned slow and sexy.

And hot.

Eventually, he was the one who took her shoulders and put her gently but firmly back in the driver's seat.

They were quiet for an endless minute or two.

Finally, so softly, she asked, "Well?"

"If you're sure..."

"I am."

"All right. Yeah. I want to be with you. It's the one single thing in all this insanity of which I have no doubt."

The visit to the E.R. took a lot longer than the talk with Jack Roper. There were piles of papers to fill out and nothing much to fill them with. There were questions about who was going to pay the bill. Tessa said she would.

Ash drew the line on that one. "Absolutely not."

In the end, although they had no guarantee that Ash would ever be able to pay, they didn't turn him away. He was led to an exam room where a nurse took his vitals and then a Dr. McKinley came in to perform an extensive exam.

The doctor, a serene fortyish brunette, said that other than the little issue of his amnesia, he seemed to be recovering from whatever had happened to him. Still, to be on the safe side, she ordered a CT scan.

The results showed that he had, literally, cracked his skull. And yes, there had been subdural bleeding. But he'd been lucky. "Very, very lucky," said Dr. McKinley. She had the film of his skull mounted on a light box and she pointed to the injured area. "The bleeding has stopped— you can see this right here." She traced a spot on the film. "Most of the blood has been reabsorbed."

"So I'm getting better, right?"

The doctor smiled a distant smile. "It does appear that way, yes. As to the retrograde amnesia you report, there are a number of other tests we can run…"

"And those tests will do what?"

She considered for a moment. He had the sense that she was choosing just the right words. "Frankly," she said in time, "the type of amnesia you appear to be experiencing is quite rare. It's not often a patient forgets his entire life after a brain injury."

He asked again, "But what will extra tests do?"

"We might find out more…"

"'More' meaning…?"

"Mr.…." She remembered he had no last name. "Ash. I think for now, we can wait."

"Wait for?"

"Your body seems to be doing an excellent job of healing on its own."

He almost laughed. "So I've been trying to tell everyone."

"It's possible and even likely that over time your memory—or a good portion of it, anyway—will return." She flipped to yet another page of the ream of paperwork they'd had him fill out. "I see that you've recalled some of your past already…"

"A little."

"Good, good." She peered at his chart. "You're reasonably close to us, right? In North Magdalene?"

"Yeah."

"And you have someone staying with you at all times?"

"I do. Tessa Jones. I'm…a guest at her house."

"Since your recovery so far has been close to miraculous, I think it's advisable to let nature keep on doing its excellent work for a while. At this point, I'm going to release you, with the understanding that you will call immediately if you experience any recurrence of your earlier symptoms. By that I mean headache, nausea, dizziness, blurred vision, anything out of the ordinary."

"All right."

"Don't fly unless you call me and get my okay first."

"I won't." He almost laughed. As if he could get on a

plane without ID and with no one even being able to vouch for who he actually was.

"If all goes well, I'll want to see you again in a week. They'll give you a number for my office at the front desk. Call there and ask my receptionist to set you up with an appointment. I want to be sure you continue to heal as you have been. Next week we'll discuss further testing and treatment." Another of those distant smiles. "And that's it. For now. Unless there's something else you want to talk about…"

As far as he was concerned, there'd been way more talking than necessary already. "No. I'm good."

Tessa was waiting in the reception area when they let him out.

She stood when she saw him, her sweet face a portrait of hope. And concern.

He went to her, wrapped her in his arms, whispered, "I'm all right. They want me to see the doctor again next Tuesday, for a checkup. That's all."

She clung to him and whispered fervently, "I'm so glad. So relieved."

He stroked her silky hair, thinking that the whole unnecessary trip to Grass Valley, the endless stack of paperwork, all of it, was worth it if it eased her mind.

When she pulled away, she suggested, "I think we might as well try to talk to a reporter at the *Union,* since we're here."

He only looked at her. Bleakly.

She got the message. "Well, fine," she conceded after a moment. "Enough for today."

"You have no idea how glad I am to hear you say those words."

"We do need to stop at the supermarket, while we're here."

"Didn't I see a grocery store in North Magdalene?"

"You did. It's way pricey and the selection is limited. Everyone in town comes down here to shop once a week or so."

So they went to Raley's Supermarket. Ash found it strange, to walk down the wide aisles in the attractive, well-organized store, pushing the cart, passing people with their own carts. So many people, going about their daily lives, buying groceries, going to work or whatever, all of them knowing who they were and where they belonged.

Except him.

Then they stopped at a coffee shop for sandwiches before they hit the highway. When Tessa put the money on the table for the waitress, he thought that he really needed to find a way to repay her for all she'd done for him.

It was dark by the time they got back to North Magdalene. The Victorian-style streetlights were on along Main Street, casting the old buildings in a golden light. In no time, they were out of the heart of town and turning onto Locust Street, where the dark trees loomed above and the snow had been plowed into high banks to either side. The sky overhead was clear and thick with stars.

"Beautiful night," he said.

Tessa made a noise of agreement—and then let out a moan of distress. "Oh, no."

Up ahead, there were three vehicles in her driveway. The house was all lit up.

"What's going on?"

"That's my dad's pickup. And Gina's SUV. They have

a key to the house. You know, just in case. And the big gold Cadillac belongs to—"

"Let me guess. Your grandfather."

"Right," she said grimly as she pulled in beside the SUV.

"What? You don't want to see them?"

"I'm sure everything's fine." She had yet to turn off the engine.

"Tessa, you're freaking me out. What's going on?"

"Nothing. I hope."

The door to the enclosed porch opened. A tall man emerged. In the glow from the porch light, Ash could see the man had brown hair, graying at the temples. He wore jeans and workboots and a heavy camo jacket.

"That's my dad, Patrick," Tessa said.

Behind him came Jack Roper and behind Jack, a giant guy with long red-gold hair, also turning gray. And two more men who resembled Tessa's dad. Taking up the rear was Oggie Jones, leaning heavily on that gnarled wooden cane of his.

Ash got the picture. "All your uncles, your dad. And your grandfather. This isn't good, is it?" A slim dark-haired woman lingered on the front step. Ash assumed she must be the stepmother, Gina. The men approached the wagon where Tessa and Ash still sat.

Tessa made another low, unhappy sound. "You're about to meet the men of my family. Oh, Ash. I'm so sorry."

Chapter Twelve

Tessa was furious with them. All of them. How dare they?

Her dad tapped on the driver's side window.

She whispered to Ash through gritted teeth, "We could just back up and drive away…."

"Not unless you want to run over your grandfather."

She glanced in the rear-view mirror. Sure enough, Oggie had hobbled on back there without her noticing. The old coot could move pretty fast when he wanted to.

And he was grinning. In the glow of her brake lights, his eyes gleamed devil-red.

"Roll down the window, Tessa," Ash said. He sounded kind of amused. Which she guessed wasn't all that surprising. After the hell he'd been through, facing four overprotective middle-aged men and one really old guy with a cane probably didn't seem all that scary.

Little did he know.

She pushed the button and the window slid down. "What?"

Her dad had his reasonable face on. Tessa knew it was just an act.

"We got worried," Patrick said.

"About what?"

Instead of an answer, he fired back a question. "Where have you been?"

She stuck out her chin at him. "To the hospital in Grass Valley. Which you should already know if you've talked to Uncle Jack." She sent a glare past her dad's shoulder at her interfering uncle, who stood back a little with her other uncles, Sam, Brendan and Jared.

"We got a little worried," her dad said again. As if she hadn't heard him the first time. "You didn't answer your phone here at the house or your cell."

"Dad. I haven't been *at* the house to answer my phone, if it's even working. Which it hasn't been since Saturday. And I forgot my cell. But everything's fine. If you'll step back from the door so I can get out of the car, we can all go inside and…have some coffee or whatever."

Her dad ignored her words—again—and nodded across the seat at Ash. "Hey. How you doin'?"

"Under the circumstances, not bad at all." Ash held out his hand.

Her father's work-roughened paw came through the open window. Tessa had to scrunch back in the seat so they could reach across her and shake. Once that was done, her dad said, "Jack tells us you got amnesia." Tessa was not the kind who hit people. But she wanted to pop her dad a good one for that, for the way he said it so casually. Like amnesia was something people got every day. On the level of a head cold or a hangnail.

But Ash wasn't offended. He shrugged. "Sad but true."

"You're starting to remember, though?"

"Yeah. Some of it is coming back."

"Well, good. How 'bout poker? You remember how to play poker?"

"Oh, no," said Tessa.

Both men ignored her. Ash said. "Yeah. I remember."

"Texas Hold' em?"

"Can do."

"That's what I like to hear. Tessa, go on inside with Gina. Your friend here is coming with us."

Ash found the whole situation humorous.

Too bad Tessa didn't. She seemed determined to protect him from her family, whether or not he needed protecting. When her dad told her to go inside, she refused to get out of the car.

Ash had to lean across and whisper in her ear. "Tessa. It's okay. I'll play a little poker, get to know them. It's going to be fine."

She searched his face, her eyes anxious. "You're sure?"

He held her gaze as he nodded.

So finally, with reluctance, she got out of the car. "You treat him right, you hear me," she growled at her father.

Her dad played innocent. He raised his arms wide to the side, as if to prove he carried no weapons. "Come on, Tessy. Settle down."

"Call me Tessy again and you won't like what I do next." She slammed the car door harder than necessary.

Then she turned and marched toward her waiting step-mother without once looking back.

Ash watched her go, thinking she was one hell of a woman and he was honored to know her.

Then the door on his side swung open and the cold night air came in and wrapped itself around him. Oggie Jones leaned in close. "Come on, son," the old man said. "You can ride with me." Ash looked into those all-knowing black eyes and wondered if he was making a mistake. Maybe he should have listened to Tessa and refused to go with them.

But it was too late to back out now.

Patrick, Jack and the guy with the long hair who Ash assumed must be Delilah's husband, Sam, took the pickup, with Jack squeezing into the back of the extended cab. The other two men got in the back seat of the Cadillac. They were Jared and Brendan, Ash found out during the short drive to The Hole in the Wall Saloon.

A tall, handsome woman with strawberry hair came forward to greet him when they all went inside. "I'm Eden, Jared's wife." She took his hand and smiled at him in a reassuring way.

"Man's got a cash shortage," said Oggie. "He's gonna need a little advance. A couple hundred oughtta do it. And if Tessy calls, you tell her we are in the back and not to be disturbed."

The place was nice and dim, with dark wood walls and round tables, bentwood chairs and a molded ceiling like the one at Tessa's store. The few people at the bar turned to look when they entered, but then quickly went back to minding their own business.

"This way." Jared headed for a green curtain at the rear. The others, including Ash, followed.

In the alcove beyond the curtain, a round table with a felt cover waited, a deck of cards and a single ashtray in the center of it. The men took seats. Oggie claimed the ashtray and lit up a cigar. Smelly gray smoke curled toward the hooded lamp above. A bartender came in, put a small stack of bills in front of Ash and took their drink orders. They all had beer or whiskey, except for Jared, who ordered club soda.

The men put their money down and the drinks came within a few minutes.

Oggie offered a toast. "Here's to you, Bill."

"It's Asher." Ash raised his beer and the others did, too. "Call me Ash." Nobody drank. They all sat there, blank-faced, with their drinks raised high.

Oggie cackled. "I coulda sworn you said your name was Bill. From Napa."

Ash looked at him steadily. "I lied. It seemed simpler than explaining how I don't know who I really am. But then your granddaughter talked me into being honest, heading over to the sheriff's station and getting with Jack, here, telling him everything I know…."

The old guy puffed on his stinky cigar. "And how'd that work out for you?"

"Looking around this table, I'm thinking I might have been better off to have stuck with pretending to be Bill."

That brought a laugh from everyone but Patrick.

Brendan said, "Well, hell. Here's to you, Ash." They drank.

"Deal," Oggie commanded, sipping more whiskey.

Jared grabbed the cards and shuffled expertly. "Cut." He slapped them down in front of Sam and the giant redhead did the honors.

Jared burned the top card and dealt them each two down.

The game had begun.

Ash won steadily. He realized quickly that he knew the game well, that he easily kept track of the cards and knew the odds of filling out each of his hands, knew when to bluff and when to play it straight, when to go all in and when to stay conservative. But the Joneses and Sam Fletcher were solid players, too. And none of them had more than the one drink they'd ordered at the first. They were all playing sharp.

Lady Luck made the difference. It seemed she sat on Ash's shoulder.

Oggie remarked on his good fortune more than once. "You're a lucky sonofagun, ain't you? Well, other than whatever happened to leave you not knowin' who the hell you are, that is." And later, "Unless you hit a losin' streak, remind me not to play cards with you again...."

After several hours, Ash had cleaned them all out. He counted out the two hundred he'd started with and left it on the table along with another hundred for a tip. Yeah, he felt marginally guilty about taking their money after they had staked him. But like all the other things he knew without knowing *how* he knew them, he understood that you didn't beat a man fair and square at poker and then insult him by offering to give his money back.

They shook hands all around. Sam even clapped him on the back.

Oggie said, "Having met some of Tessy's other boyfriends, I'm pleased to say you are a definite improvement, whoever the hell you turn out to be."

Patrick scowled. "Watch what you say about my little girl, Dad."

"Been calling it as I see it for ninety-one years and counting." Oggie blew smoke at the ceiling. "Can't see any reason to change now."

"Take my brothers on home," Patrick said in a voice that invited no discussion.

"Always glad to help," Oggie replied. They filed out into the main room, which was deserted. Only a couple of lights were on over the long, gleaming mahogany bar and the bentwood chairs had been upended on the tables. The clock above the door said it was 2:32 a.m.

The Cadillac and the pickup were both parked in front. Oggie, Sam, Jared and Brendan got into the El Dorado.

"Don't hurt him too bad," Oggie called out to Patrick before ducking into the driver's seat. "We promised Tessy we'd bring him back in one piece."

"Shut up, old man." Patrick spoke more or less automatically as he climbed into the pickup and pulled the door closed.

Feeling only slightly apprehensive, Ash got in on the passenger side.

Patrick stared out the windshield, making no move to start the engine, as Oggie gunned the Caddy's big motor, and then pulled out and drove away. The car's taillights disappeared as it turned a corner.

More silence. The street was deserted, quiet as the end of the world, the snow on the sidewalk roofs sparkling in the glow from the vintage streetlights. Even the brown road-salt slush on the pavement seemed to glitter.

Finally, still staring out the windshield, Patrick spoke. "You seem all right. I like the way you handle yourself." He turned then and leveled his gaze on Ash. "You understand, we needed to get a sense of you. Just to be on the safe side."

Ash didn't let his gaze waver. "I've got no problem with that."

"Tessa takes care of herself and does a pretty fair job of it. I know I got no right to interfere in her life. But a father has got to do what he can to be certain nothing bad is going to happen to his kid."

Ash nodded. "Makes perfect sense to me."

"I'm gonna say this, because I have to. Because this whole amnesia thing you have going on makes for what I would call special circumstances, given that there's no damn way any of us can get inside your head and know what's really happening in there. So this is what I have to tell you. You be straight with my girl, do the best you can in your dealings with her and you'll hear no complaints from me or mine. But if I find out you stole from her or turned out to be lying this whole time—"

Ash put up a hand. "I get the picture. And it's fine. It's fair."

Patrick Jones nodded. "Just so we understand each other."

"We do." The strangest thing happened then. Patrick's face faded. Ash was looking at his own father, at thick silver hair and still-black brows. Green eyes. A square jaw with a cleft, same as his own. A certain air of pride. And command.

Davis, he thought, and knew it was his father's name.

And then, in an instant, the illusion faded. He was once again staring into the blue eyes of Patrick Jones.

"Well, all right." Tessa's dad actually smiled. "We better get on back then. Those women will be gettin' riled and a riled woman is the last thing a man needs in the middle of the night."

* * *

Tessa and her stepmother were sitting at the table when Ash and Patrick entered the house.

The stepmother stood. "It's about time. We would have called the sheriff—except he was with you."

Ash's gaze went straight to Tessa. She met his eyes with a questioning look. He gave her a nod to let her know he was all right.

"Don't get on me, Gina," Patrick said in a tone gentler than any he'd used all night. "We got a game going. A game takes time."

"Oh, don't I know that after all these years?" She smiled at Ash. "Well, you've survived a night with the Jones boys. And I see you're still standing."

"I'm just fine. Thank you."

"He oughtta feel fine," grumbled Patrick. "He cleaned us out."

Tessa's eyes flashed with satisfaction. "Good for you, Ash."

Patrick reached for his wife's hand. "Come on, Gina. Time to head on home."

Tessa stood and she and Ash saw them out. Ash put an arm across her shoulder as they stood there under the porch light, waving her mom and dad off. She reached up and wrapped her fingers around his. He thought he could stand there forever, with Tessa close to his side, her fingers holding his, out in the cold winter night.

When they went back in, Ash put his winnings on the table. "It's not enough, I know, for all you've done. But at least it'll help pay my way…."

She came to him, slid her arms around his waist and

then up along the back of his shoulders. "Keep it. A man needs a little pocket change."

He kissed the tip of her nose, thinking, *So this is happiness. What do you know?* The bulldog sat a few feet away, watching them, a low, happy whine in her throat, and he felt the white cat brush against his pants leg.

"I'll keep a few bucks so I can buy the burgers next time we're down in Grass Valley." He said the words and wondered at himself. It would be a week until they drove down to the hospital again. Anything could happen in a week. Still, it was so easy to see himself here, in the small Sierra town, indefinitely. Or anywhere, as long as Tessa was there, too.

She said, "Guess what? The phone is working."

"Great. And I have more good news...."

"Tell me."

"I saw my father's face tonight. And I remembered his name. Davis."

"That's your last name, then? Davis?" Her voice quivered with excitement.

But he had to shake his head. "No. Sorry. I'm still in the dark on that one. Davis is my father's *first* name."

"You're sure?"

"Yeah. I don't know how I know that. But I do."

As always, she focused on the positive. "See?" Her eyes were green as lucky clovers, touched with the gold from the end of the rainbow. "It's coming back."

"You're right, though. I could really use a last name."

"It'll come to you. It'll *all* come to you."

"You seem so certain."

"I am." She touched the side of his face the way she liked to do.

He turned his head and kissed her palm. "Let's go to bed."

Arms wrapped around each other, the cat and the dog taking up the rear, they turned for the bedroom.

When Ash woke in the morning, he knew the names of his brothers and sisters. He reeled them off to Tessa.

"I'm the oldest," he said. "And then Gabe and then Luke, Matthew, Caleb, Jericho, Joshua—and our sisters, Abilene and Zoe." He knew what each of them looked like and he knew their personalities. And what they did, whether in the family business, or out on their own—that Gabe was a lawyer and they called him "the fixer." That Luke ran the family ranch. "I still can't remember the name of the ranch. I have a feeling I've dreamed of it. And I'm still not remembering my last name, either. I know that if I could just get the name, everything else would bust wide open."

"It'll come," she said, as she always did. "It *is* coming. You remember more every day. Call Jack. Tell him what you've found out."

Ash made the call. Jack thanked him for the update and told him to call again anytime he remembered more. "And I'll get back to you," the sheriff promised again, "the minute I have news."

They took the dog and the cat with them when they went to open the store. "They get lonely at home," she said. "And they're very well behaved." The dog had a bed behind the counter and the cat liked to sit in the front window display and watch the world go by.

The editor of the *North Magdalene News,* a bearded guy in a western hat, came in at a little before 11:00 a.m. He'd heard about Ash from Jack. He took pictures and

Ash gave him an interview. Barring a big fire or a robbery, he said, Ash would be the lead story on the *News*'s front page next Tuesday.

At 2:00 p.m., Oggie showed up with a reporter from the *Grass Valley Union*. There were more pictures. Ash gave a second interview.

"This should run in the morning edition," the reporter said. "In any case, we'll get it in by Friday."

Ash shook his hand and thanked him.

"Never play cards with this guy," Oggie told the reporter. "He may not know who the hell he is, but he can clean your clock at a poker table."

"Just lucky," said Ash, his gaze drawn as always to Tessa, who stood behind the counter ringing up a sale. She sensed his glance and beamed him a bright smile.

Oggie adjusted his suspenders. "When you've lived as long as I have, you know just about everybody. I've got contacts at a few of the Sacramento TV stations. I'm working on getting one of them to put you on the news."

"Great," said Ash. No, he wasn't all that thrilled with having his face all over the news, to be known as the guy who'd managed to lose his own memory. But the more people saw his face, the more likely that someone out there would recognize him.

Oggie made good on his promise. The next day, Thursday, he drove Ash down to Sacramento to be on the five o'clock news. Tessa stayed behind to work at the store.

The old man talked all the way down there and all the way back up. Ash didn't really mind the constant chatter. He would just throw in an interested sound every now and then and Oggie would keep right on flapping his yap. The interview was over in less than sixty seconds. Which was fine with Ash. The shorter the better, he thought.

The producer shook his hand and told him his face had just appeared on TV screens throughout the northern half of California. Affiliate stations would probably pick it up and broadcast the interview in Nevada and Oregon, as a public service.

"That's gettin' the damn word out," Oggie declared.

They got back to North Magdalene at 7:30 p.m. that night. Oggie drove Ash to Tessa's and then came in to say hi to his granddaughter. He ended up staying for dinner—and talked nonstop all through the meal. Strangely, in spite of the endless babble and the smelly cigars, Ash found himself growing kind of fond of the old guy.

When Oggie finally left, Ash and Tessa cleaned up the kitchen. He watched her bending over to put a plate in the dishwasher and he realized he couldn't wait another second to have her in his arms.

He stepped up behind her and pulled her back against him when she straightened. He nuzzled her neck, breathing in her tempting scent.

"Ash, really, we need to finish…"

He turned her around and claimed her sweet mouth.

She sighed and opened for him. Without letting go of her mouth, he scooped her up and carried her into the bedroom.

Moments later, he settled between her smooth thighs and she wrapped her arms around him. He entered her by slow degrees, claiming her body as she surrounded him.

No woman had ever felt so good, so exactly right. Again, he thanked whatever forces had brought him to her door.

* * *

Ash woke at a little after 8:00 a.m. the next morning. They'd left the curtains open through the night and outside the day was pewter gray. It was snowing, sparsely, dry flakes drifting down, some of them sticking to the windowpane.

Tessa slept on her side, facing him, her breathing soft and shallow. The bulldog snored at his feet and the cat lay curled in the cove behind Tessa's bent knees.

He would have liked to lie there forever, perfectly peaceful, with the right woman at his side. But a lot was going to change now, so he enjoyed the moment while he could.

Sometime in the night it had happened.

Like a heavy veil lifting, it had all come back to him. He didn't know exactly how or why. Maybe the lessening pressure as his body reabsorbed the blood trapped between his skull and his brain. Maybe it was simply the passage of time, that it had taken time for the shock of what had happened to him to lose its hold on him, for his real self, his life, his memories, to surface.

He knew his full name now. He knew who he was and where he came from.

Lianna…

He thought the name and frowned. But no. That was over. He'd broken it off. He pushed the thought of the other woman from his mind and concentrated on something a lot more pleasant: Tessa.

As if she sensed his eyes on her, she woke. She smiled, and then the smile became a puzzled frown. "Ash? What…?"

"I know," he said. "Not all of it. But almost all."

Her mouth formed a soft O. "What…what are you saying?"

"I'm saying my name is Bravo, Asher James Bravo. My father's name is Davis Bravo. He was the first son of seven, same as I am. His father was James Bravo, born on a ranch called the Rising Sun near a little Wyoming town named Medicine Creek. My grandfather, James, moved to Texas, won a ranch near San Antonio on a bet. My father still owns that ranch. I was raised there, raised at Bravo Ridge."

Chapter Thirteen

"Oh, Ash, it's amazing!" Tessa sat straight up in bed, disturbing the cat, which gave her a squinty-eyed glare and jumped to the floor. Tessa laughed and clapped her hands like a gleeful kid. "Oh, I knew it. I knew it would happen…" She flopped back down and squirmed in close to him.

He wrapped an arm around her and kissed the top of her head. "Ever heard of Blake Bravo?"

"Of course. Don't tell me you're related to *him?*"

"I am." His infamous relative was an American legend, right up there with Bonnie and Clyde and the Dillinger gang. Blake was best known for kidnapping his own brother's kid and claiming a fortune in diamonds as ransom—and then never returning the child. But that wasn't all he'd done in his long and nefarious life. "He was a polygamist, did you know? Ended up marrying a bunch of women, and having kids with all of them, letting each woman think she was the only one."

"That's terrible."

"Yes, it is."

"And he's a relative of yours?"

"Blake Bravo's grandfather was my great-grandfather. Scary, huh?"

"Luckily, you're nothing like him." She wiggled in even closer, tucking herself tight against him. And then she craned her head back so she could see his face. "Tell me."

He laughed. "Tell you what? My whole life?"

"Yeah. All of it. Every detail."

"Got thirty-three years?"

"You're thirty-three?" At his nod, she pressed her lips to the base of his throat. "All right, all right. Just the important details, then. You can start with what happened to you, how you got hurt…"

"That, I don't know," he confessed. "I've still got a gap of a couple of days, including what the hell hit me in the head and battered me up so bad."

She kissed his throat again. "Well, when I read up on head injuries, it said people sometimes never recall the days or hours immediately before and after they got hurt."

"Damn."

She tipped her head back once more to meet his eyes. "Still, it *could* come back at some point." Her eyes widened. "Wait!"

"What?"

"Do you remember your phone number? Your address? The phone number at your family's ranch?"

"Yeah."

"Well, then you need to start making calls. We need to—"

"Shh." He kissed her forehead. "Hold on."

"What do you mean, hold on? We can't hold on another minute. Ash, you have to know that they're probably frantic. They're probably desperate for news of you. They need to hear you're alive, to find out you're safe and well."

Her words stunned him. By God, she was right. To them, he would be missing. Missing without a trace for nearly a week. How could he not have realized that until Tessa said it? It was all too much, too fast.

"Absolutely." He took Tessa by the shoulders and put her gently away from him. "I have to call Gabe."

"Gabe…" She shoved her hair out of her eyes. "The second brother? The 'fixer,' you said…"

"That's Gabe." He snatched the phone from the nightstand and dialed Gabe's cell from memory.

He answered on the second ring. "This is Gabe."

The sound of his brother's voice stunned Ash all over again. Sweat broke out on his brow. He felt like a dead man called miraculously back to the living world.

Gabe said, "Hello? Anyone there?"

Ash found his voice. "Hey." It was rusty and rough with all the emotions swirling within him. "It's…me."

"Ash?" Astonished. Hardly believing.

"Yeah. Me, Ash."

"My God. Ash…" His brother's voice trailed off into silence.

"Gabe. Gabe, you still there?"

"Yeah. Right here. Just…shocked as hell to hear your voice. At last. It's about damn time. We've been worried. Worried bad."

"I'm sorry, I…" How to explain it? What to say? He looked into Tessa's soft eyes and decided to start with the truth. "Something happened to me. I don't know what. I've had a head injury, though I still don't know how I got it. I've just today started really remembering, where I come from, how to get hold of you, and Dad and Mom…"

"Whoa. A head injury, you said?"

"Yeah. I know it sounds crazy. But for days, I've only had a vague idea…of home, of who I am."

"You're saying you've been suffering from some form of amnesia, is that it?"

"Yeah. That's it. Hard to believe, but true."

"But you're okay now?"

"Yeah. I'm on my feet. Improving. Better every day."

"Good. You won't believe what's going on around here."

"Hit me with it."

"Bad times. Real bad times. Dad got freaked enough by Sunday to drive up to the cabin to find you, even though you'd left specific instructions that you were turning off your cell and no one was to try and contact you. You said when you took off that you'd be back by Monday. You remember that, right?"

The cabin. In the Hill Country. A family retreat. Had he gone there—or said he was going there? "Uh. No. No, I'm not at the cabin."

"We realize that. When Dad got there, he found no sign you'd ever been there. And, well, Monday has come and gone. Plus, they found one of your cars at Stinson Airport—so where the hell are you? I don't recognize the area code."

His mind felt slow. Thick. "Area code?"

"Yeah. Wherever you're calling from." He rattled off Tessa's number—from his phone display, apparently. "Is that where you are? We can reach you there?"

"Yeah. That's it."

"I'm still not getting this, man. You sure you're okay?"

"Yeah. It's a long, confused story. I'll get into detail later. But the main thing is I'm all right. And I'm damn sorry I scared everyone. Seriously. So sorry."

"What can I say? If you didn't know, you didn't know. It's been bad around here, though, with you missing. And with no one having any idea where you went or how to find you…"

"Which is just what I called to tell you. I'm in a little town in northern California. North Magdalene, it's called and—"

Gabe swore. "You're serious?"

"Yeah. What? Why wouldn't I be?"

His brother muttered, "I should have known. Northern California…."

"Should have known? How?"

A silence. Ash knew then that there was something his brother hadn't told him yet. Something important.

Finally, Gabe started to speak. But he didn't get far. "Ash, I…" The words wandered off into silence again.

Gabe was the one they always sent out to deliver bad news. He had a talent for handling the roughest kinds of situations. So this must be pretty damn bad if the family fixer was having trouble figuring out how to say it.

Tessa waited quietly beside him. He took her hand, twined their fingers together, drew strength from the warmth of her, from the steady, hopeful way she gazed at him.

He prompted, "Gabe?"

From the other end of the line, his brother spoke at last. "Right here."

"Whatever it is, I think you'd better just tell me."

Gabe swore. "Yeah. I am. You said you had a head injury?"

"Yeah."

"And you've had lapses in your memory?"

"That's right."

"So. Do you know…about Lianna?"

Lianna…

Should he have known it would be about Lianna?

Along with the rest of his life, good and bad, except for that one blank spot, Ash remembered Lianna. She was the woman in the ballroom, the one he'd dreaded facing. He could see her now, in his mind's eye: her thick coffee-brown hair, her slim, perfect body. Her big brown eyes.

Lianna Mercer, of the San Antonio Mercers. Ash had pursued her relentlessly, seeing her as exactly the wife he needed. They moved in the same circles. Her father and his father belonged to the same clubs, and had brokered any number of land development deals together.

Lianna was the perfect wife for him. Too bad the more he was with her, the more she made him want to punch his hand through a wall. Lianna had to be the star of every encounter, the center of attention, the queen of the world.

He had never loved her and that was fine with him. But as the months went by, he started to see that he didn't even like her. The closer it got to their wedding day, the more certain he'd become that he would have to break it off with her.

And he *had* broken it off, hadn't he? Yes. He was sure he had. He'd been planning to call it off for weeks. He must have told her it was over sometime during the couple of days that remained lost to him.

Then again, he wondered, how could he be so sure he had ended it when he had no memory of telling her they were through?

His mind rebelled at the question. He *was* sure. He just didn't know how or when it had happened.

"Ash. You still there?"

"I'm here. What about Lianna?"

"Are you sitting down?"

"Damn it, Gabe. Stop…handling me. Just tell me."

Tessa gasped. He realized he was squeezing her fingers too hard. Loosening his grip, he brought her hand to his lips and kissed the hurt away.

Gabe said, "There was an accident. A plane crash…"

"I don't…what?"

"Lianna was on one of the BravoCorp jets. On the way to San Francisco. It was supposed to be the two of you. You remember that, right, the trip you planned to San Francisco?"

He did remember, now Gabe said it. It was going to be a romantic getaway, just the two of them. But that hadn't happened. Because he'd ended it. He'd broken their engagement.

Hadn't he? "I remember. Yes. The San Francisco trip." It came out as a croak. His damn head was spinning. The only stable thing in the room was Tessa, sitting next to him, so still and calm, her hand in his.

"Lianna's alive," said Gabe. "You should know that upfront. Lianna's alive and the pilot and copilot, too. The plane hit bad weather, got blown off course. Went down in the Sierras. It happened Saturday morning. They were all—

Lianna and the crew—airlifted to a Reno hospital. Both the pilot and copilot have given statements. They claim that you were in the cabin minutes before takeoff. That you and Lianna were arguing. But then you got off before the plane left the ground. You aren't on the manifest."

"But, wait. Lianna…"

"Yeah?"

"She's alive, you said. She's okay. What has she said about it?"

"Ash, I'm sorry. She's not okay."

"Not…?"

"She's in a coma."

"A coma. My God."

"I'm sorry, man…"

"I can't believe it. Lianna. Damn it to hell."

Tessa made a low, sympathetic sound. He glanced at her tenderly, kissed the back of her hand a second time.

Gabe said what Ash had already figured out. "So, then. Somehow, when you disappeared, you ended up in the same part of California that the plane went down. You had injuries, a serious head wound. It's too much of a coincidence. You must have been on that plane."

Ash remembered the story on the news that first night. Of the plane that had crashed in the Sierras. One passenger, two crew members. All present and accounted for.

Except for Ash. Somehow, even though the pilot and copilot believed he'd gotten off, he must have remained on the plane. And gone down with it.

"Ash, did you hear me?"

"I heard you. And yeah. You're right. My memory's still messed up. But how else could it have happened? I must have been on that plane."

Chapter Fourteen

After the call to Gabe, Ash knew he needed to explain a few things to Tessa. But when he started trying to tell her about Lianna, she put a finger to his lips.

"Your parents. I really think you should call them next, before anything else."

So he called the big house in San Antonio. After Blanca the housekeeper got over the shock of hearing his voice, she told him his mother and father had gone to stay at Bravo Ridge. "During this so difficult time," she added softly.

He thanked her and called the ranch. His mom answered. She had just got a call from Gabe. "Asher. At last. Hold on. I'll let Gabe go and be right back. Do not hang up."

"I won't, Mom. I'm right here."

She clicked off long enough to tell Gabe she'd call him later and then she was back on the line, trying valiantly not to cry, telling him how much she loved him. She demanded he come home right away, but then she changed her mind and insisted he stay where he was. She and his dad were flying to California.

His father got on the line next to hear for himself that his oldest son was all right. Somehow, finding his father at the ranch at that hour of the day freaked Ash out more than any of it. In Texas, it was almost 11:00 a.m., on a weekday. Davis should have been at the BravoCorp building in San Antonio, kicking butt and brokering deals. Only death or disaster would have kept him away from his desk.

"Son?"

"Yeah, Dad. I'm here."

"It's true, then. You're safe. I hardly dare to believe it."

"Yeah. I'm okay, Dad. Going to be okay…"

"We're coming there, coming to you. We should be there by afternoon."

Ash told him how to get there, gave him the phone number at Tessa's house and at her store. "I'm staying with a wonderful woman," he said. "Her name's Tessa. Tessa Jones." He reached for her hand again and she shyly gave it. "She rescued me, Dad. She saved my life."

"Well, great," Davis said gruffly. "I'm glad you've been taken care of. Thank her for me."

"I will." He leaned toward her and they shared a quick kiss.

His father said, "Now, I just want you to stay right there."

"Don't worry, Dad. I'm not going anywhere."

When he hung up, Tessa asked, "They're coming here?"

He nodded. "They'll fly into Sacramento, I think. They'll be here late today."

"Good," she said. "I'll bet you can't wait to see them."

"You're right." He touched her sleep-tangled hair, smoothing his hand down it. "Tessa…" He pulled her toward him and rested his forehead against hers.

She pulled away. "Okay now." Her voice was so gentle. "Whatever it is you need to tell me, go ahead."

"At this rate, we'll be late opening the store."

"Worse things have happened." She brushed his knee through the blankets with a tender hand. "Go on. Tell me."

Suddenly he got how Gabe must have felt trying to tell him about the plane crash and Lianna being in a coma. So much to say. How to even begin?

Simple, he thought. *Keep it simple.* So he said, "I was engaged, to a woman named Lianna Mercer. It didn't work out, so I broke it off right before I ended up here, in California."

She blinked. "Um. Engaged?"

"Yeah. But it's over now."

"You're…sure?"

"Positive. Tessa. You have to believe me. There's only one woman I'm thinking of. And that's you."

She was quiet. She tucked the blankets a little closer around her breasts and folded her hands on top of the covers. "When you were talking to your brother, didn't you say something about her being in a coma?"

"Yes, I did." Quickly, he explained what he knew. About the planned trip to San Francisco, about the plane going down. About how the pilot and copilot said he'd argued with Lianna. How he wasn't on the manifest. "But somehow I must have stayed on the plane, after all…"

"Where is she now?"

"A Reno hospital."

"You, um, probably ought to go see her, after your folks get here."

"What? I told you. I feel rotten for her, sorry about what's happened to her. But it wouldn't be right to go see her. The two of us are through."

"Ash. Come on. You were on the plane on Saturday. You were arguing with her. But…you had broken the engagement before that?"

He put his hand to the healing wound on his forehead. "Look. I'm still not clear on the order of some things. But I'm positive that I broke up with her."

She stared at him. Her eyes were kind, but there was confusion in them. And hurt, too. "Did you…remember her before? And just not mention her to me?"

Honesty. A real bitch sometimes. "I remembered…that there was someone. Some woman I dreaded having to deal with. I had a dream of her standing behind me, tapping me on the shoulder. I woke up before I turned to her, before I realized who she was."

"Oh, Ash…"

"Damn it, Tessa. I didn't want to worry you, that's why I didn't tell you about that particular dream. I didn't know…what it meant. So I didn't mention it."

She said nothing. She stared down at the blankets and then, cautiously, glanced back up at him.

He commanded, "Don't look at me like that."

She started to speak. But then Mona, who had jumped to the floor while Ash was talking to his dad, started whining from her usual spot in the open doorway to the hall.

Tessa put on a fair approximation of a smile. "Mona needs to go out." She threw back the covers. "I'll take her downstairs." The sight of her naked body broke his heart.

Too swiftly, she was reaching for her robe, covering herself from his eyes.

He had a terrible feeling of absolute certainty that he'd never see her naked again. That he had found himself— only to lose the one woman for him.

Ridiculous. Not true. He said flatly, "I'll go ahead and get the coffee started."

"Good idea."

And she was gone.

When she came back upstairs, he got another forced smile. "We should get moving, huh? I'll take a quick shower. Won't be long." She disappeared into the master bath.

He cleaned up in the hall bath.

Twenty minutes later, they were both in the kitchen, throwing breakfast together. Silently. Ash knew there was a hell of a lot more to say. If only he could figure out how to say it.

They were just sitting down to eat when Jack Roper drove up in his sheriff's office SUV. Tessa got up and ushered him in. "Want some coffee?"

He took off his sheriff's hat. "I'd like that."

So Tessa poured him a mug and he joined them at the table. "We've got big news," she said. "Ash has remembered his name and, well, pretty much everything. He's called his parents in Texas. They'll be coming out today."

Roper sent him a cool look. "Congratulations."

"Thanks."

"Your last name wouldn't be Bravo would it?"

Tessa choked on her coffee. "Uncle Jack. How did you know?"

"Woman in Reno just woke up from a coma. She was in a plane crash, private jet went down up near the summit last Saturday, near Gold Lake Road. The woman's name is Lianna Mercer." He raised his mug to Ash and drank. "While you were remembering everything, you happen to remember her?"

Ash refused to drop his gaze. "I remember her. So, then. Lianna's okay?"

"She's getting there. She claims you're her fiancé. And that you were on the plane with her when it went down."

Tessa hardly knew what to think.

Everything seemed to be happening at once. Ash knew who he was. And his parents were coming.

And there was a woman named Lianna who'd just come out of a coma. A woman who said she was engaged to him, though Ash claimed he wasn't, that he'd broken it off—although he wasn't sure when the breaking-up had happened.

Tessa knew he wanted to talk more about it. So did she. But really, what else was there to say?

Either he and Lianna Mercer were engaged.

Or they weren't.

And whether they were or not, well, it didn't seem right. It didn't seem…settled, between Ash and the other woman.

The other woman. Tessa almost laughed. Because really, if there was an "other woman," wasn't Tessa it?

Ash helped her out at the store in the morning and through the early afternoon. Business was slow, as usual, because it was the middle of winter. They had a number of opportunities to talk undisturbed. But they didn't.

Neither of them seemed to know what to say, how to begin…

His father called at 2:00 p.m. to say they'd taken one of the family jets to Sacramento, as planned, and had arrived at Executive Airport there a few minutes before. They were renting a car and should be in North Magdalene within a couple of hours.

Private jets. Tessa tried to take that in. His family owned jets. Plural. One of them had crashed up near the summit last Saturday, but they still had another to spare.

She was getting the picture, painfully clear, that he was the first-born son of a rich and powerful Texas family. Yes, she'd had a feeling that when his memory came back, he'd turn out to be a guy who'd done all right for himself. But the Bravos—and Ash with them—had evidently done considerably better than all right.

Which was great. Wonderful. And also somehow strange and disorienting.

At a little after 3:00 p.m., Ash left the store to walk back to Tessa's house. He would be there, waiting, when his parents arrived. They'd have a couple of hours to themselves, a private family reunion, before Tessa got home.

Tawny Riggins came in at 3:30 p.m., glowing with love and happiness, her pale hair so pretty, soft and wavy to her shoulders. "Tessa!"

Tessa rushed to her and they hugged. "You're home…"

Tawny pulled back enough that they could grin at each other. "I can't believe it. A week and a day and I'll be Mrs. Parker Montgomery. I swear, I never thought it would happen."

"Parker here, too?"

Tawny and her fiancé lived across the Golden Gate Bridge from San Francisco, in Sausalito. Their small house wasn't far from the mansion where Parker's family lived—including Parker's sister-in-law, Faith, who was a Jones by birth.

Tawny nodded. "He's here with me. We're staying straight through to the wedding."

"A week from tomorrow. Yikes. Time does fly."

"And tomorrow night's my bachelorette party. You're still coming, right?"

"I'm there. You know that. Wouldn't miss it for anything." They were taking over the back room at The Mercantile Grill—Tawny and her bridesmaids and several of her other girlfriends from town.

"And Tessa…" Tawny was looking at her sideways, a gleam in her eyes. "I've been hearing things. About a guy. A total hunk who's been staying with you. As usual, the stories are all over the place. They say he's your boyfriend Bill, from Napa. And then they say he's not Bill at all."

"Not Bill. Bill and I are so last week."

"Then…?"

"Ash. Ash Bravo." Right then the bell over the door rang and two middle-aged women entered. Tessa didn't recognize either of them. She lowered her voice for Tawny's ears alone. "It's a very long story…."

Tawny hugged her again. "I hear you. Later. But it's something…special, right?"

"It is. Special. Very, very special."

"I am so glad—tomorrow. Eight. The Grill."

"I'll be there."

Tawny left and Tessa waited on the two out-of-town customers. They were serious shoppers and each ended up spending several hundred dollars on gold jewelry and handmade quilted jackets and wool peasant skirts. It was 4:40 p.m. when Tessa rang up their purchases. She watched them head for the door, thinking that Ash's parents were probably at the house by now, wishing she could be there to greet them, but knowing it was probably better for them to have a little time with him alone.

The two customers had no sooner gone out the door than the bell rang again and Oggie hobbled in, smoking a cigar.

"Get that stinky thing out of here, Grandpa."

He grumbled, but he went back out and stuck it in the sand-filled ashtray not far from the door.

When he came in again, he turned the Open sign around.

"What are you doing?" She marched over to the door and flipped it back the way it was supposed to be. "I am open until five-thirty and you know that. I can't just go turning the sign around any time I don't feel like customers. If I did, I'd be out of business in no time."

Oggie grumbled some more. "Man can't talk with his own damn granddaughter in private these days...."

She threw up both hands. "We're alone. Talk fast."

But Oggie did nothing fast. He hobbled over to a chair in the corner, shooed Gigi off it and took his time settling in, putting his cane in easy reach, huffing and puffing as if the effort it took to get comfortable exhausted him. He stretched out his bandy legs in front of him. "All right," he said at last. "Something's up. I been to see Jack, who's got his sheriff's attitude on. All he would tell me is that Ash's last name is Bravo and his parents are comin' to town today. I know there's more. I'm here, so you can tell me everything."

So. Jack wasn't talking. Tessa felt relief. She did not want the Jones boys going after Ash for having a fiancée he'd somehow failed to mention. She'd figured Uncle Jack would keep quiet now he knew his niece wasn't in any physical danger from the stranger she'd rescued. It was good to know she'd figured right.

"Start talking," Oggie commanded.

She gave him a fond smile. "I love you, Grandpa. Mind your own business."

"I think you should invite me over for dinner tonight. I want to meet Ash's folks."

"Grandpa."

"What?"

"No. Get it? No. You will meet them, I promise. Just…for tonight, leave it alone."

"Humph. Well. Guess you made that clear as a poke in the eye with a burning stick."

Half an hour later, after insisting she go in the back and make him some coffee and prodding her mercilessly to change her mind and tell him every last detail of what was going on with Ash, Oggie gave up and hobbled out the door.

By then it was 5:15 p.m. She was anxious to get home and meet the Bravos. She was hoping they would like her, worried about the woman named Lianna, already missing the magical days she and Ash had shared alone together.

Everything seemed to be happening so fast suddenly. Too fast—well, except for the last fifteen minutes until closing. Those minutes dragged on forever.

Finally, 5:30 p.m. came. Tessa turned the sign around, put the cash in the safe and the cat and the dog in the wagon, locked up and drove home, where the lights were on and a big, silver Mercedes was parked in her driveway.

In the house, Ash and his parents were sitting at the kitchen table. They rose when she entered.

His mom smiled. "Tessa. It's so good to meet you."

Aleta, who was tall and slim with thick brown hair, hurried forward.

Tessa shooed Mona into the hallway and put Gigi down just as Aleta reached her. She looked into the woman's blue eyes—eyes like Ash's, so vivid. So deep. And she knew that here she had a friend.

Aleta hugged her close, whispered, "I cannot tell you how grateful we are. Thank you, thank you."

"I'm…so glad you're here." She looked past Aleta's shoulder and smiled at Ash's father. Davis Bravo nodded, but he didn't smile back.

When Aleta let her go, Ash said, "Well, you've met my mom. And this is Davis, my dad."

"Hi." Tessa stepped forward and stuck out her hand.

Davis took it. Now, he smiled, but it was a cool smile, one that didn't reach his eyes. "Great to meet you, Tessa. Thanks for saving my son's life."

She kept her head high. "I'm just glad that everything has worked out, that Ash has found his family again. That he and everyone else on that plane—" *even Lianna Mercer* "—are going to be all right."

The evening was…strange. Tessa put together a simple meal and Ash opened a bottle of wine. They ate. Aleta asked Tessa about her family and her life in North Magdalene. Tessa made her answers brief. There was so much that the Bravos had to catch up on. She learned that Ash was CEO of the family company, BravoCorp. BravoCorp was mostly in land development, but they also had oil wells in the Gulf of Mexico and various investments they managed all over the country and in South America.

Ash. A CEO.

She sent him a glance. And he gave her a warm smile. Something in her expression must have bothered him. A slight frown formed between his straight black brows.

But then his father said, "We thought we could drive up to Reno tomorrow and see Lianna. Rachel's there, looking after her, so we'll see how she's holding up, too."

Aleta explained to Tessa, "Rachel is Lianna's mother. She and I went to UT together, in Austin, years and years ago."

"Ah," said Tessa, her throat clutching. She swallowed. Hard. They were driving to Reno to see Lianna.

And I will not, under any circumstances, burst into tears.

Ash spoke then in a low, controlled voice. "Dad. I told you earlier. It's over between Lianna and me."

Davis sipped his wine. "Ash. You've been through a terrible experience. It's natural you would be somewhat confused."

"No. Not confused. Not on this. Not confused in the least."

After that, the men were silent. It was a grim, extended silence. Tessa and Aleta tried to keep the conversation going. They talked of the weather and Tessa asked about the family ranch.

When the meal was over at last, Ash said, "Tessa. We should take Mona outside, don't you think? That dog needs a walk."

The last thing Mona Lou ever needed was a walk, so what he meant was that he wanted a few minutes with Tessa alone. She felt absurdly dewy-eyed at the idea, even with the way his father looked at her like she was some evil fiancé stealer.

Davis frowned and started to say something, but Aleta put her hand on her husband's arm. "We'll just get settled in upstairs, then," she said. "Thank you so much for the lovely meal, Tessa."

Ash helped her into her purple jacket and put on the one she'd given him from the store. They bundled up in gloves and hats. And finally, they took Mona and went out.

"And where does Mona want to go?" Tessa asked him as they reached the driveway, Mona waddling along behind them.

"Down the road toward the highway." He took her hand. "Don't pull away," he said softly. It was a threat, though a tender one.

They left the lights of the house behind and moved into the shadows of the trees. Maybe twenty feet along the dark road, he turned to her. He captured her face between his gloved hands.

She caught his wrists, took his hands away and stepped back. "No. I'm sorry. So sorry. But…you have some things to work out. We both know that you do. We can't just pretend you don't."

His eyes gleamed, dark as night. A low growl of frustration rose in his throat. "It's over with her. How many times do I have to say it?"

"Ash. Please. Just…let's look at this logically."

"Logically." He swore and turned away.

"If you did break up with her—"

"If?" He whirled back, pinned her with a hard glare. "Damn you, Tessa. What is this? You don't believe me, either?"

She put up a hand. "Poor word choice. I'm sorry. What I'm getting at is that you remember everything now, except for about, what, thirty-six hours before the plane crash and maybe an hour or two after it?"

"Yeah. So?"

"So, you don't specifically remember breaking it off with her, but you're certain that you did. That means you had to have ended it at some point during the time that still hasn't come back to you."

"And this is significant because…?"

"It's just that everything's happened so fast. Too fast, I think. According to my Uncle Jack and your dad, Lianna still thinks you're going to marry her."

"She's lying. Or maybe she doesn't remember, either. She's been in a damn coma."

"When were you supposed to be married?"

"Valentine's Day. Does it matter?"

"Oh, Ash." She didn't know why that made it worse. But it did, somehow. Valentine's Day, the day for lovers. It was less than a month away. "Was it going to be a big wedding?"

"Enormous." He said the word with distaste.

"I'll bet your fiancée's been planning it for a year."

"Longer. And Lianna is not my fiancée. Not anymore."

"It's a lot to break up, Ash. A wedding like that. All that goes into it. And then there are your two families, how close your parents are to hers. Whatever Lianna's like as a person, this has got to be awful for her." A tear got away from her and trickled down her cheek.

"Damn it. Tessa. You're crying. Crying for *her*…" He tried to reach for her.

She didn't allow it. "Listen to me. Please. This time we've had…it's been so special. So precious and wonderful. I'm grateful, for every moment I've shared with you. But your real life has found you now. And I think that you have to…" She let her voice trail off. It sounded too much like a lecture she was giving him, on what to do, on how to live his life, now he knew who he was at last. She didn't want to lecture him. She wanted...

So much. Everything. A lifetime. With him.

Could that ever happen? There was no way to know yet. Not until he'd made peace with the life he'd left behind.

At last, he spoke. "You're right." It was an admission. "I hate it, but I accept it." Through the shadows, she saw his big shoulders were slumped, as if in defeat. "I'll go to Reno and see Lianna tomorrow, see what's going on with her. Somehow, I have to figure out this mess."

Chapter Fifteen

Ash made his bed on the couch that night.

The next day, while Tessa worked at the store, Ash went to Reno with his mother and father. They were back when she got home at 6:00 p.m. There was dinner, during which Ash and Tessa were mostly silent. Ash's mom tried to make pleasant, meaningless conversation. And Davis talked of how good it had been to see Lianna recovering, how she'd looked small and frail in that hospital bed, with that scary white bandage wrapped around her head.

"But as beautiful as ever," Davis said. "It's a hell of a relief to know she's going to be all right." He spoke to Tessa, as if she needed to know. "Her doctors say she'll be up and around in no time. Everything will be fine. Everything will work out." He sent his son a significant look, which Ash took pains to ignore.

A few minutes later, Davis started in about how eager he was to get back to Texas.

Ash said flatly, "I can't fly until I check with the doctor in Grass Valley."

"Monday, then?" his father suggested hopefully.

"I'll give her office a call first thing Monday morning, see if she can fit me in a day early."

Monday, Tessa thought. So soon. Davis had mentioned that the jet was waiting in Sacramento. They could leave Monday after the doctor visit. Or Tuesday, at the latest.

So soon. Too soon…

Tessa had Tawny's bachelorette party that night. The Bravos insisted they'd be fine on their own. So Tessa went over town to The Grill and partied with her lifelong girlfriends. They all teased her about Ash. She told them what a great guy he was and left it at that.

It was after 1:00 a.m. when she got back to the house. Davis and Aleta were in bed.

Ash had waited up. They walked down the road in the freezing darkness, side by side, but not touching. He told her that Lianna had cried and said she was so sorry that they'd fought. When the others left them alone, Ash said he had tried to get specifics out of her, to get what she remembered, what they'd said, how he had ended up on the plane when the pilot and copilot said he'd gotten off.

"But she said she didn't remember clearly, just that we had fought, just that I was with her when the plane went down."

Tessa wrapped her arms around herself against the cold—both outside and in. "She does still think you're engaged to her, then?"

He nodded. "She looked so awful, black circles under

her eyes. Weak. I couldn't do it, couldn't tell her right then and there that it's over, that it's been over for a week, whether she remembers it or not."

"Ash." She spoke softly. "It's okay. I understand…."

"I hate this."

She swallowed, whispered, "Me, too."

"She and her mother are going back home tomorrow."

"It's safe, then, for her to fly?"

"Apparently. Tessa…" He started to reach for her, then carefully put his hands at his sides. "I have to go back to San Antonio."

She smiled, though in her heart she was crying. "Of course you do."

I love you, she thought. But she didn't say it. It wasn't the right time for her to say it.

Maybe someday.

And maybe never.

Monday, Ash got the okay from Dr. McKinley to fly. And Tuesday morning, he and his parents packed up the rented Mercedes.

Once they were ready, Tessa went out to tell them all goodbye.

Davis shook her hand and gruffly thanked her for saving his son's life. "If you need anything. Ever. You give me a call." He pressed a fancy, embossed business card into her hand, even though Aleta had already given her numbers and addresses for the family ranch and their San Antonio house, and Ash had made sure she had all his phone numbers and the address of *his* place in San Antonio.

Then Aleta hugged her. "Don't be a stranger," she whispered. "Come see us. Anytime."

"Thank you," Tessa said and meant it, at the same time as she couldn't help doubting such a thing would ever happen.

And then Ash embraced her. She wished they could stay like that, arms wrapped tight around each other, forever, wished they could share one last kiss, at least.

But it wasn't to be.

"I'll come for you," he whispered. "Don't doubt me…"

She didn't doubt him. She believed in him completely.

It was only that now their time together was over, the magic and the beauty of it had begun to seem more and more like a dream. He had his real life to go back to. And she had hers, here, in her childhood home.

Tessa stood in the driveway, Mona Lou at her feet, a brave smile on her face, waving until the Mercedes was no longer in sight.

After that, she took her dog and her cat and went to open her store. It was a surprisingly busy day for a Tuesday in January and Tessa was glad for the work. It helped to take her mind off of missing Ash. Oggie stopped by in the afternoon. She told him that Ash and his parents had gone and waited for him to gripe and moan that he'd never even had a chance to meet the man's folks.

But Oggie only asked, gently, "You gonna be okay, Tessy?"

"Yeah," she said. "I'll be okay." She said the words and knew they were true. Somehow, even though her heart was breaking, deep within she felt…stronger, somehow. *Better* than before she'd known him.

Maybe real love did that, made you better, truer than before, no matter how it all shook out in the end.

Real love, she thought. Yes. Exactly. That was the important thing. She loved Ash, she'd given him her heart. No matter what happened, some part of her would always belong to him.

She cried that night, at home, with only Gigi and Mona for company. And once she'd dried her tears, she sat with the curtains open and stared at the full moon in the clear night sky and wondered if it was a clear night in Texas, too.

Ash spent Tuesday night at Bravo Ridge. The whole family was there, everyone happy that he'd come home to them safe and sound. He hugged his sisters and got clapped on the back by his brothers. It was good to be with them. They shared a toast to his return. Through the beveled glass windows of the front sitting room, he could see the full moon. It made him think of Tessa and that hurt.

"Ash. You okay?" asked his baby sister.

"Never been better," he lied through his teeth.

Wednesday, Ash went to his office at BravoCorp and tried to catch up on his workload a little. He also called and cancelled the credit cards he'd lost in the crash. He was promised that new ones would be arriving within a day or two—and reassured that no one had been using the cards since he lost them. If someone had stolen his wallet, they'd had sense enough to be content with the cash he'd been carrying.

He sat through three endless meetings. And then, at 2:00 p.m., he took off to get his driver's license replaced. Once he had the new license, he told the limo driver to take him home, where he got one of his own cars and drove to the Mercer mansion in the historic King William district. Lianna was staying there, in her parents' house, until she fully recovered from her injuries. The housekeeper greeted him and asked him to wait in the foyer. A few minutes later, Rachel Mercer appeared. She took his hands and kissed his cheek and said that Lianna was resting. Could he come back later?

He went away hating himself for feeling relieved that he didn't have to deal with his supposed fiancée that day. That night, he and his brother Gabe had dinner together at a restaurant they both liked. Gabe was good company. And he knew when to keep his mouth shut. He asked about Lianna. Ash answered with nothing but a cool look, and the subject was dropped for the evening.

Later, at home in Alamo Heights, Ash had a last whiskey alone in his study and tried not to think about Tessa. It was no good. He picked up the phone and dialed her number—and then quickly hung up before it had a chance to ring.

The next day, Thursday, was more of the same. He went to work. After that, he tried to see Lianna. That time she was "out." He told himself that was good news, if she was well enough to go out…

He called her that night. She was still "out." He left a message to call him when she got in.

Lianna didn't call.

The whole thing was getting beyond ridiculous. As if she could put him off indefinitely. What did she think? She could just avoid him until February 14th, when he'd show up at the altar to provide her with the wedding ring to match the huge engagement diamond he'd given her?

Friday morning, he got up and got out of the house at 6:00 a.m. He was ringing the doorbell at the King William house at 6:15. The housekeeper answered. He didn't wait for her to tell him that Lianna was still in bed, just wrapped his fingers around the edge of the door and pushed it wide.

"Mr. Ash!" The housekeeper fell back, dark eyes wide.

"I want to see Lianna. I do not want to be told she's asleep or out or otherwise unavailable. I'm not leaving this house until I've talked to her."

"I will…be right back. You wait here, please." The woman turned for the stairs. Ash fell in behind her. No way was he waiting around to hear how Lianna couldn't see him now.

The woman turned halfway up the curving staircase and cast an apprehensive glance back at him. "Please. Wait."

He nodded. But when she started moving again, he was right behind her. She reached the top of the stairs and started down the hallway to Lianna's room. At the end of it, she tapped on Lianna's door. When no one answered her knock, she called, "Miss Lianna…"

"Go away!" Lianna's sulky voice commanded from somewhere inside.

"But, Miss—"

"Are you deaf?" Lianna shouted. "I said go. Go. Away."

Ash listened to her being rude to the housekeeper and thought, *Drama queen.*

And that was when it happened.

That was when the final pieces of the puzzle that was his life before he found Tessa Jones fell into place.

In an instant, he saw the days he'd lost. The dinner with Lianna Thursday night, when she babbled on about what she'd bought that day and what she would buy tomorrow and the details she still had to iron out about the wedding. She called him a bastard when she realized he wasn't really listening. He'd thought how he was trapped and it was his own damn fault, that he would never get away from her. Then there was the going-through-the-motions of the next day, Friday. And Saturday morning, when he woke up and realized he was supposed to be getting on a plane with Lianna in an hour, flying to San Francisco for a romantic weekend together.

He knew then that he couldn't do it, couldn't go there. Uh-uh. No more.

He'd called his mother and told her he was heading for the cabin, that he was turning off his cell and not coming back until Monday. He hung up before she could sputter out a reply or start asking questions about why he wasn't on his way to California with Lianna. He also called his assistant Melody, disturbing the poor woman at home on a Saturday, to tell her the same thing.

And then he'd gotten in the car and headed for the Hill Country, deciding about ten minutes into the drive that running away wouldn't solve a damn thing. He needed to deal with the problem, needed to call a halt to the pending disaster that would be his marriage to Lianna.

So he went to meet her at the plane.

Ash smiled to himself. Yeah. He remembered. He remembered it all. At last, he knew for certain. What had happened, how it had gone down—all the way to the moment when he found himself lying in a snowbank after the crash, his mind blinking in and out of consciousness but clearing long enough to watch a guy in winter gear and a ski mask come roaring up on a snowmobile. Ash had thought he was rescued. But then the guy jumped off just long enough to go through his pockets and strip off his Rolex. Then the thief was back on that snowmobile, roaring away through trees.

Amazing. Mugged by a snowmobiler after a plane crash. Who would have guessed it? Ash had lain there in the snow for an indeterminate time after the guy in the ski mask rode away with his wallet and his watch. Eventually, he'd managed to get upright and somehow, he'd staggered through the snow to the highway where a kind-hearted trucker had picked him up.

Oh, yeah. Everything. He remembered it all.

And he *would* deal with Lianna now, this morning. Nothing was going to stop him. He'd been put off way more than long enough. He stepped forward, took the housekeeper by her plump shoulders and moved her to the side. Tuning out her frantic protests, he rapped on Lianna's door.

On the other side, she started shouting again. He heard her stomping closer. "What is the matter with you, Marta? I said—" She flung the door wide—and gasped. "Oh! Ash…" Her face was flushed. She wore a bronze wisp of silk. And nothing else. There were fading bruises from the crash on her arms and legs. The bandage around her head was gone. So was her hair on one side, where they must have shaved it at the hospital.

From the first door at the top of the hall, her father called, "Lianna, what the hell is going on?"

Ash stuck his foot in the way so she couldn't try to shut the door on him. He spoke softly. "We have to talk. You know we do."

"Lianna!" Her father's voice boomed again.

Lianna seemed to know she was caught. She brought her hand up to the bald side of her head. "I look awful…."

"You look fine. We have to talk."

"Lianna!" her father bellowed a third time.

"It's nothing, Daddy," she called sweetly. "It's okay. Go back to sleep…" The door down the hall clicked shut.

And Lianna stepped back, allowing him into the room. "You can go, Marta," she told the housekeeper before closing the door.

Ash stood there, staring at her. He hardly knew where to begin.

"All right." Her pretty mouth quivered. She sagged against the shut door. "Say it. Just go ahead. Say it."

They stood in a sitting room. Through another doorway he could see her wide bed, satin sheets in disarray.

"We broke up," he said. "I remember it clearly now."

"No…" She put a hand to her mouth as the tears welled and began leaking from the corners of her eyes. "No…."

"Yes." He told it as it had happened. "You were already on the plane when I got on with you. You started ragging on me for being late. I said I wasn't late. I was only there to tell you it wasn't going to work with us. I said how sorry I was, but it was over."

"Oh, no…"

"That's exactly what you said, Lianna. *No.* Over and over. You were crying. And yelling. You started throwing things from that giant shiny red bag you'd brought into the cabin with you, screaming at me, calling me all kinds of really colorful names."

"I didn't…" She was sobbing now, all pain and denial. But he looked in her streaming eyes and he saw the lie there. She *had* thrown things. And even if the head wound she'd suffered kept her from recalling the specifics, she knew he'd called it off with her. She'd been lying from the moment she regained consciousness, even though the lie was so damn pointless. Eventually, it had been bound to come to this.

Ash went on, speaking softly, patiently, "The copilot came out of the cockpit and said they were ready for takeoff. I told him I wasn't going. You dug in your heels and said that *you* were. So I asked the copilot to give me five minutes and I'd be off that plane. He ducked back into the cockpit." Ash remembered the look on the man's face. The guy had flown Lianna before and he was only too happy to get out of that cabin, to put a door between himself and the crazy Mercer heiress. Ash said, "You started ranting at me again, that I couldn't break up with you, that we were getting married and if I thought otherwise, I was very wrong."

"Ash. Please…"

"Almost done," he told her gently. "Then you pulled that bottle of Cristal from that red bag of yours…."

"No. Oh, no…"

"I didn't see you do it. I was already turning to go. You said, 'Ash. One more thing.' And when I turned back, you hit me in the forehead with that bottle." He reached up, absently, touched the healing scar. "It wasn't the plane crash that almost cost me my life. It was you and a bottle of excellent champagne." And that was why he had reeked of booze, later, when he'd forgotten who the hell he was.

"I didn't mean to do that," she cried. "I was…so upset…"

"But you did do it. And now you've admitted that you do remember."

"I…oh, God…." Sobs shook her slender frame.

He said, "I stayed on my feet. I thought I was all right. It wasn't until later, after the crash, when the blood started leaking under the bone, that I lost consciousness. But at the time, when you hit me and the champagne went flying, I just went into the restroom to clean up. And while I was in there, the plane started moving…"

"You have to understand," Lianna sobbed. "It was

terrible for me…" She buried her face in her hands and her slim shoulders shook.

He went to a fragile inlaid side table and whipped several tissues from the box waiting there. Then, with caution, he approached her again. "Here." So strange that he could speak to her kindly, in spite of what she'd done. But then again, maybe not so strange. After all, he *had* pursued her. He had wanted her for her looks and her connections, for her money and her father's influence. And he'd almost ended up getting exactly what he wanted.

She reached up and took the tissues from his hand.

He continued, "You had told the pilot I'd left the plane. So they closed the doors, told you to buckle up, and took off."

She blew her nose. Loudly. "I just wanted us to have a little time together…."

"Lianna."

She gazed up at him through brimming eyes. "Oh, Ash…"

"It's over. It was over *before* you whacked me with that bottle. You know it. So do I. And after you hit me, I considered pounding on the door and telling the pilot to take me back to the gate. But then I decided I'd leave it alone, just go ahead and fly to San Francisco, and turn around and fly right back. If you'll recall—and you *do* recall, don't you…?"

"I…I…"

"You know what? Don't tell me. I'll tell *you*. I spent the trip in the sleeping alcove, with the door between it and the main cabin pulled shut and latched, reeking of expensive champagne because it was all over me and I had no clean clothes to change into. Eventually, the ride got too wild and I came back out and buckled up and tried to calm you down again."

In the endless twenty minutes or so before the crash, the plane had lunged from side to side, shuddering, while it dropped and leveled out, rose and dropped again, keeping them plunging and bucking, worse than any airplane turbulence he'd ever known.

There was little more to say. He finished the story. "And that was it. The plane crashed."

Lianna collapsed to the floor. She wrapped her arms around her knees and curled into a ball. "I…I messed up. I know it."

He stood above her, staring down at her half-shaved bent head. Gently, he instructed, "You will tell your parents and everyone else that you realized you were wrong, to have agreed to marry me. That you know now it can never work out. You just don't love me. And so you had to break it off with me. I'll tell everyone the same thing."

She lifted her face to him, swiped the tears away— and took the giant engagement ring from her finger. "I…thank you."

She was thanking him? "For what?"

"For saving me my pride, at least, for letting me call it my choice, for not suing me for bashing you over the head the way I did…." In her big brown eyes, he saw a flicker of real understanding. Maybe there was hope for her after all. In time. Once she grew up a little. She held out the ring to him. And then she blinked. "You're not…going to sue me, are you?"

He shook his head. "Keep the damn ring. Sell it. Give it away. Whatever." Ash felt the weight of the world lift from his shoulders. He no longer had to wonder what had happened on that plane. And Lianna had finally accepted that the two of them were through.

His life was his own again. He knew himself better than he ever had before. He understood who he was and where he came from in a way he never had until now.

Most important of all, he knew where he was going.

Chapter Sixteen

In North Magdalene, Saturday dawned cold and crystal-clear. Tessa looked out her bedroom window and breathed a sigh of relief. It was a good day. A perfect day. Just as Tawny Riggins had always insisted it would be.

At 2:00 in the afternoon, in the white clapboard Community Church, Tawny walked down the aisle to marry her longtime love, Parker Montgomery.

Tawny's dad gave her away and Parker's brother, Price, was the best man. Tawny had five bridesmaids, all dressed in red velvet—including Tessa. The matron of honor, Tawny's big sister, Amy Riggins Jones, wore red velvet, too.

The bride was a vision in white satin and lace. She carried red roses, which she passed to Amy before the exchange of vows.

"I do," said the groom, his voice steady and sure.

"I do," said the bride, all the stars of the heavens shining in her eyes.

"You may kiss the bride."

And Parker took Tawny in his loving arms as everyone in the chapel erupted in cheers and joyous applause.

After the vows, they all went over to the town hall, where there was a sit-down steak dinner for three hundred, followed by dancing upstairs in the knotty-pine ballroom.

Tessa danced with her dad and her uncles, with so many of the guys she'd grown up with, most of whom were married now to women she'd known all her life.

She chatted with her sister, Marnie, who had driven up with Mark from Santa Barbara for the occasion.

"You look good," Marnie said.

"I feel good," Tessa said. And strangely, she did. She missed Ash every day, she wondered how he was, if he was well. She thought that the time might come when she'd have to head for Texas. But that time wasn't yet. Tessa confided in her sister. "I'm thinking of selling the store and trying my luck elsewhere."

"You're kidding me. I never thought *you'd* leave town."

"Oh, well. What can I say? Even your saintly big sister is capable of change."

The bride and groom cut the cake.

And then Tawny threw her bouquet. Tessa caught it, which had everybody clapping wildly. She simply turned and handed it to Marnie. "I believe this is yours."

Marnie winked at Mark. "We'll see…."

The bride and groom were leaving for their honeymoon in the Bahamas. Everyone ran out to Main Street and pelted the long, white limousine with birdseed as the car rolled majestically away from them, the beer cans tied to the back bumper banging and clanging along the street like an out-of-tune brass band.

Once the limo disappeared around a turn, they all filed back inside, where the band started in again.

Oggie hobbled up to Tessa, hooked his manzanita cane over his arm and bowed in a fashion that could only be called courtly. "Tessy, may I have this dance?"

So she danced with her grandpa, slowly, to an old song they were probably playing back when he and her Grandma Bathsheba were in love. As the song ended, Oggie announced, "I just want to say, he'd better be good to you."

She laughed, "Grandpa, what are you babbling about?"

"I never babble." He took his cane from over his arm, leaned on it, and pointed with his other gnarly hand. "Look there. At the door."

Slowly, Tessa turned as the final bars of the song faded on the air. "Ash," she whispered, hardly daring to believe.

He stood in the doorway to the landing and the stairs leading down to the lower floor. The light from the landing limned his black hair in gold. He wore black slacks and a white shirt and a perfectly cut sport coat. She had never in her life seen a man as handsome as Ash Bravo, standing there so tall and proud, his blue gaze scanning the room.

Her grandpa, shameless as always, was shooing everyone from the floor. "Go on now, step back. Give a man the space to find what he's looking for." He cleared the way between Tessa and the man in the doorway.

And then it happened. Ash saw her standing there alone in the center of the scuffed pine floor.

He came for her, in long strides, those fancy boots of his eating up the distance between them.

And then he was there, before her. And the ballroom was so silent, you could have heard a snowflake drift to the floor.

He said, "At last."

And she said, "Oh, Ash."

"Did you doubt me?"

"Not too much. Not deep in my heart."

"I'm free now."

"I know that. I can see it in your eyes."

"I love you, Tessa."

"And, Ash, I love you."

He stepped closer. And before she realized what he was up to, he'd braced a hand at her back and slid one low behind her knees and lifted her high against his broad chest, as if she weighed nothing—in just the way she knew her Uncle Sam had lifted her Aunt Delilah, to carry her from The Hole in the Wall and into their future as husband and wife.

Right then, the whole place erupted in catcalls and whistles. And Ash Bravo carried Tessa Jones out of that ballroom.

Into love. And happiness.

And the rest of their lives.

* * * * *

Watch for Gabe Bravo's story,
The Bravo Bachelor,
coming in April 2010 only from
Mills & Boon® Special Moments™

*Mills & Boon® Special Moments™
brings you a sneak preview.*

In A Fortune Wedding *it has been nearly twenty years
since the one-night fling between Frannie Fortune and
Roberto Mendoza. But now Roberto is back and
secrets of their past are about to explode into the
present – along with an ironclad love that
cannot be denied!*

*Turn the page for a peek at this fantastic new story
from Kristin Hardy, available next month in
Mills & Boon® Special Moments™!*

*Don't forget you can still find all your favourite
Supermance and Special Edition stories
every month in Special Moments™!*

A Fortune Wedding
by
Kristin Hardy

Red Rock, Texas
July 1991

"Come on, boy, come on," Roberto Mendoza muttered, crouching over the withers of Cisco, his big bay gelding, as they raced up the tree-studded grassy slope. The speed was intoxicating. The wind rushed over his skin. A kaleidoscope of sound filled his ears—the thud of hoofbeats, the rush of his own breath.

The silvery sound of laughter ahead of him.

And then they burst up onto the hilltop, the great blue bowl of the sky arching overhead.

"Hah! We beat you!" Frannie Fortune whooped, reining in her little chestnut mare and wheeling around. "Who says the girls can't outdo the boys?" With her short, sunbeam-blond hair and tilted eyes, she looked like a pixie, ready for mischief.

Life, Roberto thought, just didn't get any better than this.

"You girls only won because you took a shortcut," he told her.

"Don't blame us because we're smarter. We just took a faster way."

"Yeah, like straight up the side of the hill."

"Admit it, you're impressed."

He grinned. "I am, but next time you decide to take your shortcut, leave me with a suicide note for your uncle. I'm supposed to be watching out for you."

Her cheeks were still flushed with the excitement of the race. "I keep telling Uncle Ryan I don't need looking after. So I got thrown once. It can happen to anyone. You try staying in the saddle when a killdeer flies up between the feet of that monster you're on," she challenged. "See how you feel when your fanny hits the ground."

Roberto's lips twitched as he slid off Cisco. "I guess you'll have to come to my rescue."

"If you're lucky." She gave him an arch look.

How had he ever thought her standoffish? It hadn't been that, but simple shyness that had kept her quiet and to herself when she'd first arrived at the Double Crown Ranch where he worked. As the weeks had passed, she'd blossomed, quiet diffidence giving way to a sly humor that perpetually hovered around that delicate mouth, the surprisingly bawdy laughter that burst out of her more and more often as the days went by.

Maybe it was just being here, out on the ranch, amid the rolling terrain of Texas hill country. It could make anybody happy, although he might be biased. No matter where his life took him, Roberto thought, no place would ever feel as right as this patch of territory where he knew nearly every tree, bush and bird by name. It was in his blood, as much a part of him as his brown eyes.

Frannie walked over to stand next to him. "You think you'll ever leave here?" she asked, as if she knew what he'd been thinking.

He watched as she bent down to pick a long stalk of grass. "I'd have to have a real good reason. I figure I'll save my money, buy a place of my own someday."

Living and working out on the land, he couldn't imagine anything better. Certainly not sitting all day in a college classroom, no matter how much his father wanted him to. José Mendoza hadn't taken the news of his twenty-year-old son dropping out well. To avoid skull fractures from the two of them butting heads in the family's restaurant, Red, Roberto had come to work at the Double Crown, where his uncle Ruben Mendoza ran operations for the Fortune family.

And where the lovely, coltish Frannie had appeared for a visit just days later.

Too bad she'd somehow gotten snowed into dating Lloyd Fredericks, the original self-important, silver-spoon guy. But she was a Fortune and he was a Fredericks, so maybe they did belong together. It still set Roberto's teeth on edge every time he saw Fredericks drive in to pick her up. The jerk didn't deserve a woman like Frannie.

"So, what are you going to call your ranch?" Frannie interrupted his thoughts. "The Rocking RM? The Double R?"

"I was thinking Red Oaks."

"How about the Slowpoke?" she offered.

His eyes narrowed. "Remind me again who won when we raced last week?"

"That's because you had an unfair advantage," she argued. "Cisco's two hands taller than Peaches. We had to outsmart you."

What she'd done was about stop his heart when he'd seen her tearing up the side of the hill. She might have started out quiet and shy, but she was fearless now.

"You just got lucky this time," he said.

"No, I was prepared," Frannie corrected him, twirling her grass. "Lloyd says that's what luck is, just opportunity meeting preparation."

"That sounds like your boyfriend. Always looking for an angle."

She rolled her eyes. "He's not my boyfriend. We're just going out. Anyway, I don't want to talk about Lloyd. You buy Red Oaks and I'll come to visit." She gave him an impish look. "And Peaches and I will beat you then, too."

He reached out and swiped the blade of grass from her hand.

"Hey," she protested.

"You need to learn some respect for your elders."

"My elders?" She snorted. "You think a fancy new hat makes you all grown-up?" That all-too-delectable mouth of hers curved.

Roberto eyed her. "You got a problem with my hat?"

"I don't know, but maybe you do." And quick as a flash, she swiped the black Stetson and dashed away, squealing.

He sprinted after her. "Oh, you're gonna be sorry."

"Big talk," she scoffed, clapping the hat on top of her

head. She was willow thin and fleet, feinting one direction and dashing the other, making him give chase until both of them were laughing and out of breath, circling the red oak that crowned the top of the hill.

"Give it up," he told her as they faced off on either side of a stand of piñon.

She glanced over to Peaches as though judging her distance. "Not a chance." She faked one way and he mirrored her, faked the other. And then she went just a fraction too far and he whipped around the tree and caught her, snaking an arm around her waist to draw her in.

"That's it, *chica,* you're in for it now," he growled.

"Oh, yeah? What are you going to do to me?" There was humor in those soft blue eyes, and mischief and glee. And under it all, something else, something that started the blood rushing in his veins. He caught a hint of scent that made him think of spring and sunshine. He could feel every breath she took. His pulse thundered in his ears.

She wasn't even out of school yet, he reminded himself. He worked for her uncle. He had no business kissing her. Even as his lips hovered over hers, he made himself release her.

And then Frannie leaned in to press her sweet, warm mouth to his.

SPECIAL MOMENTS™ 2-in-1

Coming next month

FORTUNE'S WOMAN by RaeAnne Thayne

Ross had his hands full trying to clear his sister's name and look after his nephew. Then Julie Osterman stepped up to help and Ross couldn't resist the lovely counsellor's appeal.

A FORTUNE WEDDING by Kristin Hardy

Years had passed since the one-night fling between Frannie and Roberto. Now Roberto was back, their past secrets exploded into the present – along with a love that couldn't be denied.

REINING IN THE RANCHER by Karen Templeton

Johnny Griego is blindsided to discover his ex-girlfriend is pregnant. Always responsible, Johnny proposes to Thea. But Thea wants happily-ever-after, not a marriage of convenience...

HIS BROTHER'S SECRET by Debra Salonen

He thought he could arrive in town, make amends for the secrets he kept, then leave. But when Shane Reynard sees Jenna Murphy again, his past longing for her is resurrected...

HEALING THE MD'S HEART by Nicole Foster

To help his sick son, Duran Forrester would do anything. Then he crossed paths with paediatrician Lia Kerrigan, who has a little TLC for father and son alike!

WELCOME HOME, DADDY by Carrie Weaver

Annie knows her baby deserves a father he can count on. So she's ready to believe that the missing-in-action soldier who fathered her son is dead. Until he shows up on her doorstep...

On sale 19th March 2010

Available at WHSmith, Tesco, ASDA, Eason and all good bookshops.
For full Mills & Boon range including eBooks visit
www.millsandboon.co.uk

SPECIAL MOMENTS™

Single titles coming next month

THE BRAVO BACHELOR
by Christine Rimmer

For Gabe Bravo, sweet-talking young widow Mary into selling her ranch should have been a cinch. But the stubborn mum turned the tables and got him to bargain away his bachelorhood instead!

THE NANNY SOLUTION
by Teresa Hill

Audrey had only been hired to look after Simon's tiny daughter's dog! But Simon was the perfect boss – and now his patience and understanding might just prove impossible for Audrey to resist.

AN IDEAL FATHER
by Elaine Grant

Cimarron is reluctant to become guardian of his orphaned nephew. But headstrong, gorgeous Sarah James knows he'd make a great dad. Can this flawed man become an ideal father?

NOT WITHOUT HER FAMILY
by Beth Andrews

Kelsey is trying to prove her brother's innocence – and creating nothing but trouble for Jack Martin, chief of police. Jack should steer clear, but he's finding Kelsey fascinating…

On sale 19th March 2010

Available at WHSmith, Tesco, ASDA, Eason and all good bookshops.
For full Mills & Boon range including eBooks visit
www.millsandboon.co.uk

2 FREE BOOKS
AND A SURPRISE GIFT

We would like to take this opportunity to thank you for reading this Mills & Boon® book by offering you the chance to take TWO more specially selected books from the Special Moments™ series absolutely FREE! We're also making this offer to introduce you to the benefits of the Mills & Boon® Book Club™—

- **FREE home delivery**
- **FREE gifts and competitions**
- **FREE monthly Newsletter**
- **Exclusive Mills & Boon Book Club offers**
- **Books available before they're in the shops**

Accepting these FREE books and gift places you under no obligation to buy, you may cancel at any time, even after receiving your free books. Simply complete your details below and return the entire page to the address below. You don't even need a stamp!

YES Please send me 2 free Special Moments books and a surprise gift. I understand that unless you hear from me, I will receive 5 superb new stories every month, including a 2-in-1 book priced at £4.99 and three single books priced at £3.19 each, postage and packing free. I am under no obligation to purchase any books and may cancel my subscription at any time. The free books and gift will be mine to keep in any case.

Ms/Mrs/Miss/Mr ———————— Initials ————————

Surname ————————————————————————

Address ————————————————————————

————————————————————————

———————————————— Postcode ————————

Send this whole page to: Mills & Boon Book Club, Free Book Offer, FREEPOST NAT 10298, Richmond, TW9 1BR

Offer valid in UK only and is not available to current Mills & Boon Book Club subscribers to this series. Overseas and Eire please write for details.. We reserve the right to refuse an application and applicants must be aged 18 years or over. Only one application per household. Terms and prices subject to change without notice. Offer expires 31st May 2010. As a result of this application, you may receive offers from Harlequin Mills & Boon and other carefully selected companies. If you would prefer not to share in this opportunity please write to The Data Manager, PO Box 676, Richmond, TW9 1WU.

Mills & Boon® is a registered trademark owned by Harlequin Mills & Boon Limited.
Special Moments™ is being used as a trademark.
The Mills & Boon® Book Club™ is being used as a trademark.